AF574940

ISLAND OF GOLD

ISLAND OF GOLD

James Grant

WALKER AND COMPANY
NEW YORK

To Carolyn

All the characters and events portrayed in this story are fictitious.

First published in the United States of America in 1978 by the Walker Publishing Company, Inc.

Published simultaneously in Canada by Beaverbooks, Limited, Pickering, Ontario.

ISBN: 0-8027-5400-7

Library of Congress Catalog Card Number: 78-62355

Printed in the United States of America

10 9 8 7 6 5 4 3 2 1

ISLAND OF GOLD

Chapter One

I stood quite still, my right arm at full stretch and looked into the round black hole in the end of the Colt .45. I started to count slowly and had almost reached one hundred before the barrel of the revolver began to waver. First a gentle trembling then a violent, wild shaking.

I dropped my arm to my side, rocked forward and rested my forehead against the cool glass of the mirror. After a time the roaring in my ears stopped and I decided I would, in future, have to avoid staying after hours at The Imperial Standard. I turned away and put the plastic and aluminium revolver back into its cardboard packing and added it to the pile on the floor, and then I walked slowly back to the mirror and looked at myself critically.

I was beginning to look my real age – forty two, which was an improvement. Until recently I had looked ten years older than that. I couldn't account for the improvement, as far as I could see there was nothing to justify it. I was broke, my partner Tony Miller was broke, we were behind in the rent on the shop and the state of the H.P. on the van didn't bear thinking about. I looked at my watch and wondered where the hell Tony was at eleven o'clock in the morning. I decided he was probably still in bed with one of the incredible women he somehow managed to pull almost every night. How anyone with bright red hair, freckles, slightly thyroid eyes and a habit of burping at the end of almost every sentence could prove to be that attractive to women was beyond me, but then at the time it wasn't a matter I cared to dwell upon.

Tony Miller was one of the very few of my former acquaintances who had ignored my little spot of bother and he had been the only one to offer me a job. As it turned out he needed my capital, pathetically small though it was, but it didn't matter, I needed the job more. Or rather jobs. Tony called himself a General Dealer, a euphemism in most cases and certainly in his. He bought and sold anything and although he usually stayed on the right side of the law he never let it become an obsession with him. At the present time we were selling imitation weaponry; plastic, wood and metal replicas of guns, pikes, swords and most other forms of mayhem. Made in Spain and imported by Tony and me, with any luck they would take over from three flying ducks as the principal form of suburban semi interior decor, and then we would make a fortune – or that, at least, was Tony's theory. In the meantime we shunted them around the countryside, pushing them into department stores, and the like, with a lack of success that discouraged me but left Tony unmoved. But then he hadn't been moved when we had failed to sell any of the woven plastic rugs we had imported from Tai-wan, or when we had been forced to dump God knows how many tons of frogs legs we had bought cheap in France only to find that they were cartonned, not tinned, and went rotten before we found a buyer. Then there were the second-hand cars, the accommodation agency and a few other ventures we had tried and failed at during the two years of our association. No wonder we were always broke.

The morning dragged on and just after midday Tony appeared with a hard-eyed Scandanavian girl in tow and almost as quickly disappeared across to the pub for his lunch. About one-thirty I came to the conclusion that I was hungry and, as Tony carried what little petty cash we had in his pocket, I went across after them and let him buy me a pint of bitter and a hot meat pie. The landlord of The Imperial Standard, Paddy Kinsella, was an Irishman with bad breath and no sense of humour, but he kept a benevolent slate which more than made up for his other shortcomings. He came over to our table and whispered in Tony's ear as I demolished the last of my lunch. Tony nodded, waited for me to finish and then glanced at the blonde. "Go and have a pee," he told her, which will give you as close an insight into his manners and methods with the ladies as you're likely to get.

After she had gone, uncomplainingly, he leaned forward and burped slightly. "Two fellers in the bar want to talk. Some kind of deal. Cash. We need that." I didn't argue.

He nodded at Paddy and a moment later the two men who wanted us came over. Neither of them displayed any outward signs of great wealth but I didn't let that worry me. I usually guessed wrong about such things; I was always doing jobs for people who looked rich right up to the moment I asked for my money.

One of the men was thin and about five feet nine. Sandy hair and a matching complexion made an accurate estimate of his age difficult, but I guessed middle forties. A very large moustache, also sandy, almost saved his face from being nondescript. His eyes were grey green and set deep into his face. He had a vaguely military look about him, nothing concrete, but there all the same. The second man was younger, I guessed about four or five years younger than myself. He was dark and hard and his brown eyes had almost no expression at all. I knew the type; I had known men like him most of my life, usually to my cost. The older man shook Tony and myself by the hand. The dark haired man didn't bother with a greeting and simply sat down and looked at us with brooding menace that bothered me but which Tony appeared not to notice.

"Gentlemen. A pleasure to meet you. A drink?" We ordered more beer and waited. No one spoke until Paddy had gone back to the bar. Then the older man raised his glass. "Your good health." We grunted in unison and drank. Toasts were unusual in our circle along with most of the other little niceties of life. "My name is Potter and this is my partner Mr. Delaney. I believe you gentlemen can help us with a certain transaction. You make regular trips by road to and from Spain carrying goods here for your business and wherever possible taking casual loads there." It wasn't a question so we waited. "We have such a casual load. Not here. It is in France. We want it collected and delivered in Spain. Simple." He stopped and this time he seemed to want a reply so I made one.

"Why us?"

"Why not?"

"I asked my question first." Potter grinned slightly beneath his moustache. Delaney looked as if he would have preferred to hit me with a bottle but I had already decided that he was there for his muscle and Potter was the man to talk to. I waited again.

"The load you will collect is very valuable. To us. Not to anyone else. It is also quite legal. Nothing to cause you concern."

"That doesn't answer my question. Why us? There are hundreds of people who could do that for you. Not just here but in France too. If it's all above board why come raking round here for us? We're nothing special." I knew Tony was making attempts to send me telepathic messages but I ignored him. He would take any job. Not me. I might not be all pure and white but at least my one short prison sentence had had the desired effect; I had no intention of going back. I looked at Potter who was staring into his drink. "Well?"

"Quite right. I misjudged you. There is something special about the load. Attempts will be made to steal it from you. You may be called upon to take fairly decisive action."

"Such as?"

"Nothing too dramatic. No guns. Nothing like that. Perhaps a small amount of, er, persuasion and a lot of hard driving." I looked at Tony. As I expected, he was looking slightly less enthusiastic than he had been. Violence wasn't his scene. Not that it was mine any more, not since the army had decided it no longer required my services. I turned back to Potter and wondered why he still hadn't answered my question.

"Go on," I told him.

"When is your next scheduled trip to Spain?"

"Next week. Tuesday."

"Good. Perfect. Very well, this is what is required. En route you detour to a small town near Limoges. A place called Eymoutiers. There you will collect a load of cartons and packing cases. They contain paintings and various other works of art. Some are fragile, all are extremely valuable. I assure you that none are being sought by the police. You can examine everything before you load up thus assuring yourselves that they are all I say they are and no more. You will deliver them to my customer in La Coruña. That is all."

"And who is likely to cause the trouble?"

"I am an agent for an American collector. Apart from being excessively wealthy he is also given to certain childish practices. One is that he indulges in a contest with another American, equally rich, who also collects. They vie with one another for acquisitions. This has gone on for several years. Recently they have begun to bring in variations to make life more exciting for them. They try to steal one another's latest finds. No one gets hurt. At least not physically. The men who will try to steal the load from you are under strict instructions not to harm the carriers, whoever they might be." I looked at Tony again. He had started to look interested again. He also seemed to believe the story he had just heard, but then he always had been a sucker for an unlikely tale, probably because he told so many of them himself. I thought it was time for another question.

"How much?" Potter glanced at Delaney but if it was from relief that I appeared to have bought his story I couldn't tell.

"Four thousand pounds."

"Paid when?"

"One thousand now, the remaining three thousand when you get back to London."

I thought for a moment.

"What if we get to, where did you say? Eym. . . . . ."

"Eymoutiers."

"What happens if we get there and decide we don't like the deal?"

"You back out and nothing is lost."

"And the thousand advance?" Tony asked the question.

"You keep it." I hoped my face didn't show it but that removed any shred of doubt I might have had. Whatever Potter was up to, it wasn't the operation of a benevolent society.

"We'll think about it. Where can we reach you?"

"We'll be here. Day after tomorrow, same time." I nodded and they went.. Tony followed them. I sat at the table and waited for him to come back.

"What did you tell them?"

"What?" I repeated the question slowly and not unkindly.

I liked Tony. "What did you tell them?"

"I just said. . . . . well. . . . ."

"You told them we'd do it, didn't you?"

"For Christ's sake Tom. Four thousand quid. We won't make that all year the way we're going on. We need it and you heard what he said about the job. It'll be money for old rope." I thought about it for a moment. There didn't seem to be a lot of point in telling him the whole thing stank. He wouldn't have believed me. Anyway, there didn't seem to be any reason why we couldn't go to Eymoutiers and look at the load, and earn ourselves an easy thousand pounds. Which just goes to show that in my own quiet way I'm as mercenary as Tony. And just as stupid.

Chapter Two

I had hoped we would reach Limoges before midnight but heavy rain reduced visibility and there was a lot of traffic, particularly on the stretch between Calais and Paris, and I settled for an overnight stop at Châteauroux. In the morning I dragged Tony out of bed earlier than was usual for him and he complained incessantly for the next half hour as I ate breakfast. From the map it seemed that the better way to Eymoutiers would be to take the Montluçon road turning south at la Châtre. That would bring us to Eymoutiers direct and after we had loaded up, if we loaded up, it was only a short run to Limoges and we would be back on our route again.

The police car stopped us halfway up a hill just outside Bourganeuf. It seemed routine as far as my French allowed me to understand and I followed them happily along to their checkpoint. The checkpoint was just off the road in a large barn-like building. There were three of them and they inspected our papers and then they looked at our empty Ford Transit van. They examined it very carefully and they didn't seem at all surprised when they found a small oilskin wrapped package taped inside the oil sump cover. I felt sick. Tony didn't look very happy about it either. Then they unwrapped the package and I stared at the white powder; the sick feeling was replaced by sheer panic. I didn't have to be told what it was. I had seen enough movies to know all about heroin.

It was obvious I suppose. I was so sure of the phoniness of Potter's story that I had centred all my attention on the load that awaited us at Eymoutiers – or rather didn't await us there. The load would be as unreal as the white powder that now lay on the table between us and the police was real. Once we had agreed to look at the load then Potter must have arranged for the package to be hidden in the van. No doubt there would have been a diversion waiting for us at

Eymoutiers, no load, just a diversion while they removed the drugs and then they would have let us go on to Spain. We would have been no wiser; just relieved that we didn't have a load to carry and happy that we were a thousand pounds richer. Clever. But we had been stopped. We had suffered the bad luck of a random check. The barn began to take on the air of a funeral parlour as we sat and waited for something to happen. No one talked to us. Not that I felt much like talking and Tony certainly didn't.

It seemed like hours and possibly was before anything very much happened. When it did it was unexpected. We heard the sound of a car and then voices as three men came into the barn. The first looked as if he was another policeman. The other two were Potter and Delaney. I looked at them with my mouth open and so did Tony. Potter began talking before he reached us which was just as well.

"Are these the men? If I can have a few words with them. Ensure they understand fully what is happening." The policeman who had stopped us nodded, and Potter sailed across the room as if he owned France. He waved away the lowly gendarme who was guarding us and smiled tightly. I tried to smile back but the result was not very satisfactory.

"What. . . . ." I started to say but he cut in sharply.

"You are Mr. Stanway?" I played along.

"Yes, and this is Mr. Miller."

"Good. You are aware that this is a very serious matter?" He moved closer and lowered his voice. I glanced at Delaney who was chatting to the man they had arrived with. The other representatives of law and order wandered off, presumably for a smoke. "Sorry chaps. Never mind, we'll have you out of this in no time at all." He moved away before I could start to ask the questions that needed asking and went into a muttered conference with the law. After several minutes of this he came back smiling cheerfully.

"Very well, we're off."

"Where?"

"Limoges, then with any amount of luck we'll have you away before night."

"How? What have you told them?"

"Later." He walked away again and I started to follow

him but one of the policemen wandered up and I changed my mind.

He was as good as his word and we were released into his custody just before midnight. He had booked two rooms in a small hotel in a back street and Delaney took Tony into one and Potter took me into the other. I had run out of patience and I asked for an explanation before the door closed.

"Not tonight old boy, it is rather late."

"Yes tonight and I don't care how late it is, I want an explanation. First, who put the stuff in the van?"

"Very well. Yes, we used you and you were unlucky that's all."

"No it isn't all. So you used us, that I can understand. I don't approve and very likely when I get out of this mess I will take you apart for it, but I don't understand any of the rest of it. How come we were stopped? Was that a random search? And how did you get us away from the police? The French aren't dummies. If they thought they had their hands on some international drug smugglers they wouldn't hand them over to the first person to come along. And for that matter how did you happen to come along?" I had another thought. "Anyway what are you doing smuggling drugs from England to France? That's the wrong way round." Potter sat down on the edge of the bed.

"Dear me," he said, "how very astute. Very well Mr. Stanway. I can see that you will not rest until all is resolved to your entire, well, I hardly think satisfaction is the word. But at least I will tell you everything." He lit a cigarette and smoke drifted up to the ceiling as he went over to the door, opened it and peered outside. Apparently satisfied there were no gendarmes listening at the keyhole, he started to speak again. "As you suspect you were set up. We put the package in the van and then tipped off the French police who picked you up and found the stuff. We were following and came along at the appropriate moment. Our authority is sufficient to satisfy the local police."

"Your authority?"

"Yes. We have a certain, shall I say, official standing."

"You're police?"

"Not exactly, but near enough to make no difference in this kind of situation."

"But why?"

"We want you to do a job for us Mr. Stanway. We will pay you and pay you well but, had we asked outright, there is no doubt you would have refused. Now that is unlikely."

"Why?"

"Because if you do we shall tell the French police to go ahead and in due course you will doubtless be sent to prison for a very long time." I was beginning to feel slightly dazed. Potter seemed to take pity on me. He smiled and said quietly. "I really am very sorry about all this but there is a vitally important matter that needs prompt action. There are only one or two people who can help us. You are one and as I have already indicated you were not likely to volunteer. We had to coerce you."

"What is this vitally important job that needs me?"

"Later. For now I merely want to be sure you fully understand the alternative." He blew a lethargic smoke ring. "Help us and we will get you off the hook. Easily. We will produce evidence that you were unwitting carriers. That will be that. Fail to help us and you will be left to the French. Miller too. I would guess that the length of the sentence the French will give you will be at least twenty years and French prisons are well outside the standards set by the Michelin guide." He smiled at what he doubtless took to be a little joke and sat waiting for my answer. He didn't have to wait very long.

"I haven't a lot of choice have I?"

"Not really, no." He stood up. "I will tell you the rest in the morning," he said. At the door he looked back. "One of us will be outside the door all night. The police are watching the window. Don't do anything silly." I didn't need telling. I lay on the bed for an hour thinking. It didn't do me any good. None of it made any sense at all, least of all the part about me being of vital importance to something the police, or whoever it was Potter represented, wanted doing.

As far as I could recall my life had been ordinary to the point of being dull. Ordinary school followed by an ordinary job, an apprentice in a garage, then two years National

Service which had taken me to places I would never have got to on my own. The life had seemed good and I stayed in when my time was up. I managed to get a commission at the time when the army was dragging itself into the second half of the twentieth century and giving commissions to people who deserved them rather than those whose foreheads and chins sloped at the approved angle. Then I had married and very soon after that I had found that my ability to comply with the basic tenet of two can live as cheaply as one was decidedly suspect. I went rapidly downhill and eventually I made one or two unauthorised withdrawals from the wallets of brother officers. I was caught and shot out on my ear. The worst part of that had been the knowledge that all the sloping-chin wonders and the choleric old colonels had at long last had their worst doubts and suspicions heartily confirmed. Then unemployment followed by a bit of civilian stealing, a short stretch inside and then out to more unemployment, despair, one calculatedly ineffective attempt at suicide and then Tony Miller. Needless to say somewhere along the line I had reverted to my bachelor status. Not that Christine had objected to my criminal activities; it was this lack of success which had really concerned her. That was almost all. If there was anything there that could be of use to Potter and his friends I couldn't see it and my hour's thought had given me a headache.

In the morning Delaney sat and watched us eat breakfast. Or to be exact, drink it. For once I joined Tony on his coffee only diet. Potter appeared as we were forcing down the third or fourth cup; the French can't make coffee as well as they think they can. He sat down at the table and beamed cheerfully.

"All set? Good, we'll be on our way."

"Where?"

"Don't worry about that," he told me.

"Last night. . . . ." I began.

"Later." He told me and his eyes flicked at Tony and back. That confirmed one thing. Whatever it was I was in, it didn't have a part for Tony, except that, if I didn't play ball, he suffered with me.

We were driven to a small airfield just outside the town.

A light plane was waiting for us and we took off immediately. From occasional glimpses of the sun I reckoned we were heading south. Later we turned south-east and when we touched down I was fairly certain I knew where we were. I had been there once during my army days when an aircraft I was in had landed for refuelling. The place was Istres, about fifty miles north-west of Marseilles and I remembered it being in the middle of a flat, bleak region that was wonderful if you were an ornithologist and awful if you were anything else. I wasn't an ornithologist.

Potter was well organised. He had arranged for two small huts to be allocated for our use. There were no guards this time. They didn't need any. There wasn't anywhere to go and by now I knew the odds were against me. As for Tony, nobody had told him anything and, although he wasn't showing it, he was clearly getting worried. He knew that I was deeply involved in whatever was going on and he wasn't and that probably bothered him most. Tony liked to be at the centre of things.

We ate together though and that seemed to make him happier. However, after we had eaten he was sent into solitary confinement in the other hut and Potter told me to sit down and listen. He didn't need to, by then I was burning to know what it was I was being pushed into.

Chapter Three

Potter had lit a cigarette and blown three smoke rings before he was ready to begin.

"In 1954 you went into the army for your period of National Service. You were posted to Habbaniyah in Iraq. When you were due to come out you signed on as a regular and stayed there for another three years." He looked at me to see if I was impressed. I wasn't, since I assumed he had access to records and it was all there. "While in Iraq you participated in an experimental exchange with the Iraqi army. You and three other British soldiers were seconded to the Iraq Military prison in Baghdad." He paused again and this time I was impressed. That would be on record too but only on local command records, hardly important enough to have gone onto central records. He seemed to want a reaction so I nodded.

"That's right. The idea was that they would learn from us about how we dealt with offenders. I suppose the reverse was expected but I can't say I learned very much."

"Perhaps not. The unit you were in was small. A captain, a warrant officer, two sergeants, three corporals, including you, and forty men. The other three who went with you on detachment to the prison were Warrant Officer Stancil, and two privates, Kennedy and Archer."

"Yes." I couldn't help the note of respect creeping in. He really had done his homework very well indeed.

"On and off you were at the prison for a year. You know it well?" It was a moment or two before I realised the last remark had been a question. For the first time I began to get an inkling of the direction in which we were heading — and I didn't like it very much.

"I knew it, yes. That was twenty years ago. It will have changed."

"Oddly enough it hasn't. Not much anyway."

"Well?"

"We want you to go there."

"Where?"

"We want you to go to the military prison in Baghdad. You and Delaney. Once there you will effect an entry and release a prisoner the authorities are holding and bring him out." He stopped and waited, as if to let me think. I did. Rapidly. I came to an inescapable conclusion and I didn't see much point in keeping it to myself.

"You're out of your mind," I told him. He smiled easily and let another smoke ring drift up to the ceiling.

"Not really. I realise it isn't quite as simple as that. There are a number of details to be worked out." He could have said that again.

"It isn't possible," I told him politely. "Nothing short of an army could do what you want doing."

"I think you underestimate your capabilities."

"Look, I couldn't have done that twenty years ago, I certainly couldn't do it now."

"Ah yes, your recent history does leave something to be desired doesn't it. You have gone downhill, the nervous collapse, the suicide attempt. Not very effective that, was it? A small bottle of pills followed by a quick telephone call to the doctor. Cries for help, social workers call that kind of thing." He had succeeded in annoying me and I let it show.

"Call it what you like, that has nothing to do with this. It's impossible and you know it and I won't have any part of it." Potter looked at me for a moment and then leaned forward and all pretence at amiability slipped away.

"You are forgetting something Mr. Stanway. This isn't a game we are playing. You have no choice in the matter. You do it or you go to prison for a very long time. Remember what I said, twenty years in a French prison is not a very nice future."

"It's better than no future at all."

"Is it? Are you sure? Remember you haven't heard the rest of the deal."

"I don't want to hear it."

"Don't sulk. You will be very well paid for your efforts. Fifty thousand pounds in any currency you like paid into any bank in any country in the world." I looked at him. All at once his hare-brained scheme had taken on another dimension. "Ah, I see I have your interest at last. Yes, fifty thousand pounds and of course your freedom. You will be cleared with the French police and so, of course, will Mr. Miller." I couldn't help but be interested.

"What about Miller, how is he involved in this?"

"Not at all, except as added pressure; your sentimentality towards your friends, few as they are, has not gone unoticed. He will remain outside the operation and he will have no idea what is going on. When it is over he will be released with you. Of course, he is not on the payroll. If you wish to share your good fortune with him that is up to you."

"And if it all goes wrong, as will very likely be the case?"

"Negative thinking Mr. Stanway, negative thinking. But if you mean Mr. Miller, he will be released should that unlikely event occur. He will be very mystified, but I expect his relief will outweigh his curiosity."

He was right there.

"And the money?"

"You will have no use for it if you don't come back and you have nobody to leave it to. Nobody. Unless you have some misguided ideas about a charitable organisation."

"If I don't get back you can pay the money to someone I nominate?"

"We can yes, but who, Mr. Miller?"

"To my ex-wife." For the first time I had said something he had not been prepared for and an odd expression flitted across his face.

"Well, well, well, your sentimentality runs deeper than we thought."

"Well?"

"Agreed."

"Alright let's hear your plan." He seemed slightly relieved at my acquiescence which surprised and heartened me. I was surprised that he appeared to need me so badly and heartened because I thought that, if he was so desperate to have me involved in his wild scheme, he would be less likely to watch me as carefully as he might, which would improve my chances of getting out before we reached the point of no return.

"The plan is simplicity itself," he began. "The man we want is a German national. His name is Altmann and he is being held in the top-security wing of the prison. You and Delaney will get him out." I looked at Delaney who seemed unmoved. He was either incredibly confident or he had no real idea of what was involved. Potter was going on. "You are both dark complexioned and with a little make-up will pass, your Arabic is fluent. Delaney cannot speak the language at all but no matter. Papers can be provided and you will. . ."

"Wait," I interrupted, "these are details, let's start at the beginning. How do we get into the country?"

"We will travel from here to Kyrenia in Cyprus. There we change planes. The new aircraft is a Cessna 180H Float-plane complete with long range fuel tanks. At cruising speed that gives us a range of about twelve hundred miles. Not much margin for error but enough."

"Pilot?"

"Me."

"Flight plan?"

"Take off from Cyprus will be in the early evening, eighteen hundred hours to be precise. I shall head east along the northern coast of the island to the end of the Cape of St. Andreas, from there we fly east-southeast into Syrian air-space until we are over Palmyra. Then we follow the Tripoli-Kirkuk oil pipeline; we will be flying low using extra landing lights I have had fitted. When the pipeline crosses the Euphrates we turn into a south-east heading until we reach the lake at Habbaniyah. I'm afraid it will all have to done done by dead reckoning but I'm rather good at that." He smiled his easy smile again.

"How long to when you put us down on the lake?"

"At cruising speed, about five hours."

"What is the cruising speed of the Cessna?"

"According to the book just under 150 miles per hour."

"You're joking. We might as well be standing still. We'll be a sitting target for anyone who cares to take a shot at us, from the air or from the ground." Potter was unmoved.

"That is to our advantage. We will be slow but very low and mainly over open desert. The countries we will be flying over all have fairly advanced but not too sophisticated radar installations. We will be too low for them."

"I'm not so sure about that. Iraq is not too much of a problem, as you say, most of the route is over open desert, but Syria is very touchy these days."

"The same thing applies. We will be flying very, very low. Hedge-hopping. If there are any hedges to hop."

"Alright," I said slowly, "assuming we don't hit a telegraph pole and assuming we don't get shot down what happens then?"

"As I said, I will land on Lake Habbaniyah, in the southwest corner. You and Delaney go ashore and from there. . . ."

"Wait a minute. What happens to you?"

"I keep on going old boy. Same course all the way down to Kuwait. I shall land on the bay just north of the town. Arrangements have been made for refuelling. From there I shall fly back to the lake at seventeen hundred hours the following day. If you are not there I go back to Kuwait, refuel and make the same trip every twenty four hours for the next five days."

"And then?" I had to ask even though I knew the answer.

"If we're not out in five days we come out the hard way or not at all." Delaney had answered as if he was talking about a stroll round the park. I decided against disillusioning him for the moment. If things went my way he would never find out just how hopeless it all was. Instead I asked another question.

"Assuming we are out on schedule, you plan to pick us up at the lake?"

"Yes," Potter answered, "and then come back the way we went in." I thought for a moment and, as I ran over the problems in my mind, I was suddenly aware that I was thinking seriously about the whole crazy idea. I was being sucked along with the tide. I made an effort to restrain myself but I still had to play along with them until I had a chance to get me and Tony out.

"How do we get into and out of the prison?"

"You will carry papers that will show you to be senior intelligence officers from the Iraq military attaché in Bonn. No one will know you but they won't expect to. You get to

Altmann and get him out. By force if necessary." I looked at him carefully, if he was as mad as his words suggested, he didn't show it.

"By force?"

"Yes. Does that worry you?"

"More than it appears to worry you. You did say there will be just me and Delaney. Against the guards of a military prison and God knows how many other soldiers at the barracks in and around the city. How are we supposed to beat them?"

"Surprise and hostages." Delaney replied to my question and I didn't like the answer. Not so much at what he had said but at the way he had said it. He meant it and worse, he believed it. "It will work," he said as if he was reading my mind. "There is one thing about Arabs, they have made the use of hostages common currency. They understand the terms and they will deal on that basis. If you take hostages from among the senior staff officers and, if possible, from civilian employees at the prison, they won't let them get shot for the sake of one foreign prisoner."

"Alright," I said, "let's assume for the moment that we get into the country without being shot down, which is unlikely, and let's assume we bluff our way into the prison, which is equally unlikely, and then get out with Altmann and hostages, which is even less likely, what then?" Potter didn't seem put out by my lack of enthusiasm.

"You make your way back to the lake and, as I said, I pick you up and fly you out the way we go in." I realised part of the plan was missing.

"How do we get from the lake to Baghdad? It's between fifty and sixty miles."

"You walk. You will carry a second set of papers. You will appear to be artisans on leave from one of the oil pipeline installations. On your way to the big city to blow all your pay."

"Two sets of papers? And guns presumably?"

"Yes."

"We wouldn't fare very well in a police check."

"You will have to avoid one then, won't you." It was just like the mock battles and war games we had played in the Army. Everyone sitting around calmly discussing the impossible as if it were commonplace. I decided it was a good moment to show them how weak their crazy idea was, even in its finer details.

"If we have just been paid why are we walking?" Delaney asked suddenly.

"That's alright," I told him, "everyone does. Thumbing lifts is a natioanl pastime. There's a bus service between Baghdad and Damascus but it's infrequent. And expensive."

"Well?" asked Potter.

"If we go back to the lake," I said, "we have several problems. Someone is bound to hear the Cessna going in and we must assume a report is made to the authorities. If it is and then a prison-break occurs someone is sure to be bright enough to put two and two together. They could put a guard on the lake area or simply keep an airborne watch. You would be target practice."

"Do you have a better idea?" I did but I restrained myself.

"How good are you at flying," I asked him, "to be precise, how good are you in a Cessna?"

"Very good." The answer was quiet and firm and I reckoned he meant what he said.

"Right. When we are out of the prison with Altmann and the hostages, we will demand transport, a jeep or a truck. We can easily give the impression we are planning a long drive by demanding large supplies of food, water and petrol. The natural assumption will be that we are planning to go overland. With hundreds of miles of desert in which to pick us off, they may relax their guard at the beginning."

"Maybe. If they do, so what?" Delaney sounded sceptical.

"Leaving Baghdad there is a good road running almost due south. If we take that they will think we're heading for the Gulf States. About seventy miles out there is a small town, Hillah. It stands on the Euphrates. At that point the river is wide – wide enough for a Cessna." I looked questioningly at Potter.

"Possible," he said thoughtfully.

"Somewhere along that road we can lose any trail. Don't worry about how, it can be done."

"Alright lets assume that is what we do. What about the

pick-up?"

"Only one attempt. Any dry runs and the whole thing is given away. You come in once and pick us up. If we're not there you give up and go home. We figure out another way to get back."

"Where does that leave us?" Delaney sounded less happy than he had before.

"It leaves us to do what they will think we plan to do. Go out by road to the Gulf."

"And what are the chances of that succeeding?"

"Not good," I told him. Delaney grunted and looked at Potter. I could see that Potter liked it a lot better than his partner did.

"You can give me details of the river?" he asked.

"Yes, enough, the approach you can work out yourself." He nodded and stood up abruptly.

"Very well." He walked to the door and then paused. "From this moment until we are on the float-plane either Delaney or I will be with you at all times. One false move, the slightest attempt to escape and you will be shot. Understood?" He didn't bother waiting for my reply, which was as well, I didn't have one and even if I had I wouldn't have made it. He had meant what he said. I looked at Delaney and there was the same implacable air about him. All at once I knew, crazy as the plan was, impossible as it had to be, they were going through with it. And it looked as though I was going with them.

We were in Cyprus early the next morning and Delaney hadn't taken his eyes off me for an instant. Tony had tried to talk to me before we left and had been unceremoniously pushed aside. He was left in the hut at Istres with an uncompromising looking Frenchman Potter had spirited from somewhere. He wasn't very happy about seeing me go and I wasn't all that delighted at leaving him behind. So long as he had been there a faint air of reality had persisted.

We reached Nicosia airport before nine and the pilot of the light plane that had ferried us all the way from Limoges took off again before we had left the customs building. We took a taxi to Kyrenia and were there in time for lunch. Potter disappeared as soon as we had eaten, apparently to check over the Cessna. Delaney and I sat out the afternoon in a room at the Kyrenia Palace Hotel. About four Potter came back and we ate again although by then my appetite had diminished. The three of us changed clothes and washed and shaved. All we were taking with us were bundles of other clothes and water bottles and some oil-skin wrapped packages I didn't care to think about. Potter left first and Delaney and I followed about ten minutes later. I could see the Cessna as we walked down to the jetty. Almost new, the tiny aircraft was immaculate, its bright yellow paint sparkling in the late afternoon sunshine and reflecting in the clear water. I could see Potter talking to a woman in a white suit and a large floppy white hat. Halfway down the steps I stumbled and brushed against a man in his sixties who was walking the same way as we were. He turned and for an instant I looked into a pair of cold, savage eyes before he turned away leaving an impression of a slimmer version of Erich von Stroheim, but with an air of feral viciousness about him that would have made the old actor look more suited to a children's movie. Then Delaney hurried me along and I forgot about the man. When we reached Potter the woman in white had disappeared and we climbed aboard the Cessna.

It was exactly six o'clock when the mooring rope was released and Potter taxied slowly out from the shore. I looked out of the window and on the jetty I saw the man I had stumbled against. He was standing close behind the woman in white. This time she had taken off her hat and I could see her face quite clearly. She was without doubt the most beautiful woman I had seen for a very long time. Tall, slender, with a near perfect figure, she followed our departure with interest. As I watched her I saw the man with the cold eyes move to her side and take her arm almost proprietorially. She turned and I saw her teeth flash whitely in a laugh and then they walked together back along the jetty, the slim and beautiful woman with the slightly built older man. I watched them go. She was very, very lovely and she was also the biggest bitch I had ever met in my life. I should know. I had been married to her for four years.

Chapter Four

We took off into a darkening sky. Potter kept the aircraft at about one thousand feet until we were well clear of the Cape of St. Andreas and I felt the gentle pressure as he banked onto a new course and simultaneously reduced height. From the flight plan we had discussed I knew we were then on a setting that would take us over the Syrian coastline near Latakia. We were scheduled to cross the coast at seven and right on time I felt the slight dip as Potter brought the small floatplane down to a level that didn't bear thinking about. I closed my eyes, but that only made me feel sick. I decided that feeling sick was worse than feeling frightened out of my wits and opened my eyes again and peered into the darkness outside. Fortunately it was impossible to tell what the terrain was like but soon I could feel the aircraft climbing and I knew we must be over Jebel el Ansariya. Somewhere off the port wing was a four and a half thousand feet peak and I hoped that Potter's navigation was as good as he thought it was. Gradually the aircraft descended again and one major obstacle had been passed.

The windows in the Cessna had curtains and there was a further curtain behind the pilot's seat. With them all pulled across we were able to switch on the cabin lights without making ourselves as conspicuous as a Christmas tree. Delaney and I applied each other's make-up, little more than some instant-tan cream really, but on top of our naturally dark complexions it had the desired effect. We looked dark enough to pass in that light, but what we would look like in bright sunlight would be another matter. That done we discussed whether or not to change our clothes at that moment. We decided against it, there would be time later and there was always the possibility that we would have to abort. At least, I was hoping there was still that chance. We switched off the cabin lights and drew back the curtains. Potter was not using lights, his theory was that lights were more likely to attract attention than the noise of the engine. Right or wrong, it did nothing for the state of my nerves. I checked my watch and saw that it was ten minutes to eight, that placed us over Palmyra and nearing the pipeline. I could see a cluster of lights below us that seemed to suggest Potter's navigation was everything he had claimed afterall. Moments later he switched on the landing lights and there, directly below us and frighteningly close, were the shadowy tubular shapes of the oil pipes. Potter turned his head slightly and spoke for the first time since we had taken off.

"How about that old boy." He sounded pleased with himself and I suppose he had reason to be.

We followed the pipeline for over two hours, our speed was constant and our height varied only slightly to accommodate the contour of the desert. We had decided that over open desert with only the occasional and probably unmanned pumping station to pass over, we would be safe using lights. That way we could stay low, well out of the scan of any radar station we might fly near. Shortly after ten o'clock Potter switched the lights off again and brought the Cessna up to a slightly safer altitude. Moments later he made a course correction and I knew that we were over Al Haditbah and within an hour of touchdown. I signalled to Delaney and, struggling in the confined space, we changed out of our clothes and into the stained overalls and working boots which Potter had provided and which in theory would let us walk unmolested from the lake to the city. Delaney nudged me and I saw that he had kept his boots off and was rolling his trousers up to his knees. I hastily took my boots off again and rolled up my trousers and bundled the boots inside the old topcoat I would wear on the walk into the city. Delaney was doing the same and in addition he had opened the oilskin wrapped packages. Two almost new Beretta M1951 Automatic Pistols and enough ammunition to fight a war. I hoped it wasn't an omen.

The Cessna lost height again but Potter kept the lights off. We were too close to our destination to risk being seen. We were also well inside the range of the radar installation on Habbaniyah Plateau Airfield but, by keeping low, we would be below their ground level and thus below their scanner base. Below I knew the Euphrates was winding through the desert and suddenly the light cloud cleared and in the moonlight I could see the gleam of water ribboned below.

"That's helpful," Potter remarked, "should be able to get in without using lights at all." Minutes later he pointed ahead and peering over his shoulder I could see the lake glistening in the sharp white light from the now bright moon. Potter was right, he did not need lights and he put the Cessna onto the surface of the lake with a sure hand.

I couldn't make out our exact position but after Potter's performance during the previous few hours I had no doubt that we were precisely where we were supposed to be. He taxied the Cessna as close inshore as he could risk, then switched off the engine. In the silence Delaney opened the door and lowered himself into the water. As the only swimmer of the two of us, it had already been agreed that he would go first.

His head reappeared in the doorway.

"Fine," he called, "I'm standing on the bottom. Hand me the gear." I handed out the change of clothing, boots and guns and finally two water bottles. I turned to Potter.

"See that you're there when we want you."

"Don't worry old chap," he answered easily, "I'll be there, just see that you are. All three of you." I clambered through the door and eased myself down into the water. It was cold. The water came up to the middle of my thighs and I waded ashore with difficulty. Delaney was already dressed and I hurriedly followed suit. As soon as we were ready Delaney waved to Potter who immediately started the engine and moved out towards the middle of the lake readying himself for take off.

With Delaney close behind me I scrambled over the sharp but crumbling mica-like rocks. Bright moonlight shone on the creamy white stone making the whole area far more luminous than suited our purpose. Behind us the Cessna surged over the water and lifted up into the sky. The roar of the engine filled the quiet and then gradually faded as Potter headed towards the Gulf.

"Christ," Delaney muttered, "with all this light and that

bloody racket we'll have everybody between here and Baghdad on our necks."

"Shut up," I snapped, which surprised Delaney. It surprised me too, but having taken the initiative I pressed it home. "From now on we're on our own, on this stretch we do it my way. Our chances are slim to begin with so do as I say and keep quiet." Delaney didn't answer but started moving again and I took his silence to indicate that for the moment at least we were doing it my way. I had no illusions about Delaney and I knew that if we got Altmann out of prison and on board the aircraft then in his eyes I would be supernumerary. I would have to tread very carefully indeed. We reached the edge of the rocks where the sand was deep enough to keep our movements silent but not so deep that walking was difficult. We set off along the southern shore of the lake and made good time so that within an hour the bulk of the building that was my first landmark loomed black against the sand and light-coloured rocks.

It had been built as a hotel by Imperial Airways before the Second World War, then the lake had been used as a staging post for the old Empire Class flying boats on the run to India. In my days, the R.A.F. had used it as a leave centre and the handful of soldiers stationed there were also allowed to use it.

A few lights were burning but from a distance it was impossible to tell whether they were room lights or security lights. I held up my hand and crouched, waiting for Delaney to come up to me.

"The road is between us and the building," I told him. "If we keep close to the road the going will be quicker and easier, but keep your eyes and ears open." I started off again and we soon reached the old hotel building. No one was about and we could see that the few lights that burned were porch and verandah lights. We moved slowly as we passed the building and soon the ribbon of road we were following began to climb towards the western edge of the plateau that bordered the lake.

Once we were at the top we moved faster but with more caution as the danger of detection was greater. About twenty minutes after we had reached the top, the road began a slight descent and I stopped and pointed into the moonlit dimness ahead.

"There's the main road, the next five or six miles could be tricky. First there's the army camp and Habbaniyah town, and then the second town. The road will probably have a fair amount of traffic, even at this time of night, so keep close. If anyone sees us keep walking, don't run and don't talk, not even to me." I set off again at a steady pace with Delaney slightly behind and to my right. It was about half an hour before we came abreast of the road leading down to the main entrance of Habbaniyah camp. Security lights illuminated the gate and the fence. I couldn't see any guards, but I had no doubt they were there. At that moment, up to the right, lights broke the skyline and I heard the engine note of a fast, heavy vehicle coming down the road from the plateau airfield. It was impossible to make it out clearly and I prayed that it was not a guard truck. I decided against hiding for although I was sure we were unobserved a false move then, if seen, would have had the camp guards on us in seconds. The vehicle rounded the bend into the main road and I could see that at least that prayer had been answered. The truck was a petrol bowser, an empty one judging from the way it was being driven, and it passed us without slowing. Then it swung to the right and went down to the camp gates.

We moved on again and steadily covered the ground between Habbaniyah and the town of Al Fallujah. We saw no one else on foot and only a few vehicles passed us on the road and we soon reached the outskirts of the small town. The inevitable dogs came out to investigate our approach but years of ill-treatment had made them curiously less agressive than their English counterparts. At my basic Arabic cursing they melted hastily away and, without pausing, we crossed the bridge and passed quickly and quietly through the town. As we left I quickened my pace, determined to cover as much ground as possible before dawn. We would then have to move slowly to avoid arousing curiosity and to avoid unnecessary effort in the heat of the day.

My recollection of the road was that it petered out a short distance beyond the bridge at Al Fallujah, but obviously some progress had been made and in the light of the rising sun I could see the road stretching far ahead.

"We'll turn off to the south," I told Delaney. "The fewer chances we take the better." We walked steadily into the desert for about fifteen minutes before I saw the corroded remains of an old car lying half-buried in the sand. Everything detachable had gone, but the shell was enough to serve our purpose.

"Here will do," I said. "When the sun is up this will give us some shade. We will suffer a bit around midday, but we'll survive." Delaney crouched on his heels and fishing under his coat he produced a battered pack of cigarettes and offered one to me.

"No thanks."

"How long do you intend stopping here?"

"Until about three this afternoon. It won't be comfortable but at least it will be safe and we can rest. If the prison is as bad as we expect we'll need all our energy to get near Altmann, let alone get him out."

Delaney grunted non-committedly and we made ourselves as comfortable as was possible and settled down for the day. I looked out at the bleak landscape already shimmering as the heat began to build up.

I wasn't looking forward to the self-imposed period of rest. I wasn't worried that we might be seen, even if we were there was a good chance we would get by, what did worry me was the prospect of inactivity. Inactivity meant time to think and thinking about what lay before us was something I could do without. I could also do without the other thoughts that were crowding into my mind. That Potter knew my ex-wife, which could have meant many things, few of them pleasant, and that Christine knew the unknown man on the jetty, were just two of them. I looked at Delaney and thought of talking to him about it, but the thought was still-born. Whatever it was I was involved in, there was nobody except me to get me out of it. And in an emergency I was my own worst enemy.

The last months in the army had proved that. I had become incapable of reacting positively. Decision-making became impossible and, worst of all in the army's eyes not mine, I began to worry about killing. Not that the modern army treats killing lightly, but it does consider that when necessary it has to be done. I found it more and more difficult to accept that I would ever do so. I even began to dislike the look and feel of guns. Playing with the imitations I imported had helped and the Beretta inside my jacket wasn't causing me too many problems. That is, as long as I didn't think about it too much.

I closed my eyes and tried to sleep but it wasn't possible. In my stomach I had a feeling, nothing more, just a feeling, that something was about to go very wrong indeed.

Chapter Five

The remains of the old motor car might have concealed us from any casual eyes but it did not shelter us from the heat of the sun. Long before three o'clock in the afternoon, the time we had set for moving on, the heat was unbearable. We sat outside the shell that had once been a 1953 Chevrolet Bel-Air, trying to squeeze ourselves into the tiny patch of shade it made. Finally it was time to move on and although he said nothing I knew that Delaney was as relieved as I was.

We had covered about two miles after leaving the Chevrolet when Delaney gripped my arm and pointed.

"What's that?" I looked along his arm. Moving towards us over the sand was a vehicle. It was too far off to identify but from the cloud of dust behind it the driver was obviously in a hurry. We were about three-quarters of a mile from the road but the vehicle was running parallel to the road heading away from Baghdad.

"Old habits die hard," I muttered, more to myself that to Delaney.

"What?"

"Old habits. Before the road was built they used this entire area as a roadway. About a mile wide. The driver must prefer it to the nice new road over there." By then the vehicle was very close but I was still unable to identify it. "Looks official, if it stops just sit there and smoke and look stupid and for Christ's sake don't start shooting even if it looks bad." Delaney nodded and grinned humourlessly.

The vehicle was heading straight for us and I was finally able to identify it as an elderly Austin Gypsy. It arrived with a rush and stopped suddenly, it's attendant cloud of dust blowing forward and completely enveloping it. When the dust cleared we were in trouble. One man stood against the bonnet and two others stood, one to our right and one to our left, about ten paces away from the Gypsy. They were soldiers, two privates and, in the centre, a sergeant. All had rifles and none of them looked like the lazy, aimless Arabs I remembered.

I stood quite still. Delaney didn't move and he crouched, smoking a cigarette, apparently staring at the ground about a yard in front of him. The man in the middle was the first to speak and he spoke in Arabic. At least we were being taken for what we looked like. He repeated the question.

"Who are you and where are you going?"

"To Baghdad."

"And your names?" I told him the names we were using.

"Your papers." I fumbled for our makeshift papers and at the same time eased off the safety catch on the Beretta. I bent over Delaney and held out a hand for his papers. I had no doubt that the safety catch had been off his pistol since he had first seen the truck and I sent up a small prayer that he had sufficient control to keep us out of a gunfight.

"You have been working at Al Rutbah." The words were a statement not a question so I said nothing. The less the three men heard of my accent the better our chances would be. "If you have just been paid off you will be carrying a lot of money." Again it was a statement. A slight but welcome wave of relief swept over me. Corruption was still alive and our progress would be that much easier as a result. I reached into the deep pocket of the dungarees I wore and produced a few dirty crumpled notes. Carefully at a very long arm's length the leader of the trio took them from me. He counted them and his expression changed. "You misunderstand me my friend, not this useless amount. Everything." He gestured to the other two who started to move towards us. At that moment the U.A.R. Air Force took an unwitting hand in the proceedings. A MIG jet fighter appeared, moving fast and very low. It was probably on the downwind leg of an overwide approach to the airfield at Habbaniyah Plateau but I didn't have a chance to think very much about it. As the aircraft went overhead trailing its shattering roar, four of us – the three soldiers and me – reacted naturally. We looked up. Delaney did not. Without moving from his crouching position he shot one of the two soldiers very neatly in the chest. I recovered fast and the sergeant who was no more than a pace away from me froze as my pistol appeared, pointing at his stomach. The second soldier had been covering me but as his comrade died he swung his rifle towards Delaney. That saved my life and cost the soldier his. Delaney's second shot was as neat and as fatal as his first. He stood up and turned towards the sergeant.

"Wait." I said.

"Why?" For a moment I couldn't answer, the sudden killings had started a chain reaction and I began to feel slightly sick. I looked at the Arab. "You have a choice," I said, "do as you are told and live. The alternative is. . . ." I jerked my thumb at Delaney.

"What are you telling him?" Delaney's voice was dangerously quiet.

"I'm offering him his life for his co-operation, we might be able to use him." Delaney thought about it for a moment before nodding his head in cautious agreement. "Was that necessary?" I asked him, pointing to the dead men.

"Yes. I don't need to understand the language to know what was going on. They wanted all the money we carried. Right? They would have insisted on a search and they would have found the guns. We wouldn't have stood a chance." I shook my head and turned back to the sergeant who looked a little less apprehensive than he had a moment or two before. He had obviously detected the slight change in Delaney's manner. With surprise I realised the man was still holding his rifle and stepping forward but keeping well out of Delaney's line of fire I took the weapon and threw it into the back of the Gypsy.

"Well what now?" Delaney didn't answer for a moment.

"We take the uniforms," he said eventually, "and him. He may be able to help us get into the prison." I looked at him uncomprehendingly.

"What do you mean? What about the papers identifying us as Army Intelligence officers?" Delaney looked at me for a long moment without speaking.

"There aren't any papers."

"What?"

"There never were. We're playing it by ear. When we get to the prison I planned to get us inside somehow even if I had to get us arrested. This way may be better."

"But what. . . . . . why . . . . . .?"

"We had no way of getting Altmann without your help. You know the prison, you speak the language and we must get him out. There was no other way we could think of. We had to present you with a situation that gave you no alternative but to help. This is it. You've no choice now. If you are found here with forged papers you will be shot as a spy. You know it. You have to help." Too many loose ends were waving at me to let much of it make sense but some of it did.

"You and Potter, you have no official status at all have you?"

"No."

"And that set-up in France?"

"Just that, a set-up. The powder wasn't heroin; it was harmless and the policemen were some local villains we hired. We had to get you here, into Iraq, with the least fuss and bother. And it worked and the only way out for you is to help with the break-out at the prison." I looked at him in silence. He read my mind again. "You still get the money, the fifty thousand. That part is on the level. Not immediately but as soon as we. . . . . ." he stopped for a moment, "as soon as possible after our return." There was another silence, longer this time as I tried, unavailingly, to make some sense of it. I couldn't, except for the part about me having no choice, that much was true.

I walked over to the first of the two bodies and removed the jacket and trousers and then did the same with the second corpse. Both jackets had small entry holes but neither of the two bullets had gone straight through. I dragged the bodies to the truck and quickly changed clothes with one of them. When I was ready I took Delaney's place guarding the prisoner while he too changed clothes. With the sergeant's unwilling assistance we loaded the bodies into the Gypsy. That done I pushed the sergeant into the front passenger seat, Delaney sat in the back, his pistol on his knee. I climbed into the driving seat and started the engine. I drove south, further away from the road, for about five miles, the desert becoming increasingly uneven with rocky outcrops rising from the sand.

Against one outcrop I stopped and with Delaney watching, the Arab and I pulled the two bodies out of the vehicle and pushed them as far under the rock as we could. I set the sergeant hunting for small rocks to pile over the bodies and I sat on the wing of the Gypsy and outlined some new thoughts to Delaney.

"With this we can be in Baghdad in less than two hours. It will be dusk then and with the papers from the bodies and with the sergeant's help we stand a good chance of getting inside at the first attempt."

"And if we don't?"

"We think again."

"If we don't get in what do you intend doing with him?" He jerked a thumb at the Arab soldier. "We can hardly kill him in the middle of the city." Slowly and for the first time since it has all begun I realised the nature of what was happening. The confusion Potter and Delaney had caused and the promise of a great deal of money had pushed from my mind the fact that, to survive the operation, killing had always been a probability. Probability had become reality and there was every chance it would continue. Reluctantly I realised that the overriding thought in my mind was not the killing but the money. Apparently my change of heart when I had been in the army had not been prompted by humanitarian thoughts. The only thing wrong had been the price. Potter and Delaney had found mine. It wasn't a very pleasant thought but there wasn't the time, and this certainly wasn't the place, to philosophise over it. Anyway, as Delaney had been prompt to point out, at that moment I hadn't a choice. I looked at the sergeant and he ceased to be a human being and became instead a problem to be viewed in a detached and cold-blooded manner.

"We'll try getting in with him." I told Delaney, "if that doesn't work we'll come out into the desert, kill him and go back in and try something else." Delaney looked at me with a tight smile on his mouth, a smile that was not reflected in his eyes.

"Okay," he said. He walked over to the Arab and motioned to him to climb back into the Gypsy. As he did so I turned for another look at the rock where the bodies were hidden.

For a few seconds Delaney must have let his watchfulness slip as, with a roar, the engine started up and a spray of sand, thrown up by the rear wheels, covered him. That gave the driver the few precious seconds he needed to put sufficient distance between us to make accurate pistol shooting impossible. It did not stop Delaney from trying though, and by a minor miracle he found a mark. The Gypsy jerked lumpily to a stop in the sand and I started to run towards it. Delaney called out and turning I saw him partly concealed behind the rock that formed the makeshift grave.

"The rifles," was all he said in answer to my questioning look. I realised that if the Arab was injured, but still alive, he had our measure in firepower. I was halfway between the vehicle and the rock and I decided that forward was no greater risk than back. In the event there was no risk at all. The sergeant was sitting behind the wheel, one hand gripping his shoulder where one of Delaney's bullets had hit him. He looked at me gravely and without fear.

I heard Delaney come up behind me and without a word he shot the soldier through the neck. The man was thrown out of the Gypsy, a fine spray of blood clouding the air behind him. I stared at Delaney in disbelief. I turned and ran round to the man's side hoping that somehow he had not died. The hope was not realised. I looked back across the bonnet of the Gypsy at Delaney.

"You bastard." He ignored me and climbed into the driving seat of the truck and waited. After several minutes, during which I succeeded in not being sick, he spoke.

"Let's go." I stayed where I was. "Now listen to me," he said. "We knew this wasn't going to be a picnic. If you expected to get through this without someone dying then you're a fool." He was putting into words my own earlier thoughts.

"The body," I said wearily, "we had better put it with the others."

Delaney climbed down as I started to drag the bloody corpse up onto the wing. He took hold of the feet and between us we manoeuvered it across the bonnet. We drove back to the rock and in silence we added the third body and covered it with stones. Using handfuls of sand we cleaned the blood from the vehicle and then climbed in and with Delaney at the wheel we headed east.

We kept well clear of the road never going within a mile of any vehicle we saw. Neither of us spoke until we were close to the outskirts of the city.

"We will have to go up onto the road now," I told Delaney. "We can run on into the streets beyond the airfield and find somewhere to leave this where we can pick it up later."

"No. We're safer in the truck. It's a military state and if we drive about as if we own the place we are far less likely to attract attention than if we go in on foot. We both look pretty scruffy and the last thing we want is an officer pulling us up for being a disgrace in uniform." I looked at him surprised at the attempt at humour. I nodded agreement. When we reached the road we turned right onto the tarmac surface. Within a few minutes I could make out the airfield buildings and soon we were passing the end of the main runway to our left. As we entered the city I had difficulty in remembering my way through the crowded streets. Most of the landmarks I remembered were obscured by forests of new buildings that had appeared since the revolution.

Slowly we made our way into the area of the city that housed the Military Prison and we decided it was time to leave the Gypsy. Taking care to remove the key and, for good measure, the rotor arm, we each took a rifle. The third rifle caused a problem which Delaney hopefully solved by opening the bonnet again and laying the weapon carefully across the engine. Then, with our pistols pushed out of sight under our borrowed battle dress jackets, we set off on foot. Within minutes we were in sight of the prison entrance and without breaking his pace Delaney walked up to the nearest guard not giving me a chance to change my mind. I had no opportunity to do other than concentrate on my Arabic as I told the guard our latest and hastily concocted tale. The combination of the stolen army papers and the air of confidence I somehow managed to convey did what we hoped. The guard decided that we should be seen by someone in authority and we were soon inside the gates and following his directions to the Commandant's office. These took us down below ground level and as soon as we were out of sight of the gate we stopped and held a hushed conference.

"If Potter's information is right and Altmann is in the top security wing then he will be on the top floor. That's four storeys above street level, so we start at the main stairs." Keeping close together and walking at a brisk purposeful pace we soon proved that what had held good in the British Army for hundreds of years held good there. If you looked as if you were intent on official business, no one took any notice. I let Delaney lead as we climbed enough flights of stairs to put us on the third floor level. That left one flight still to climb but the main staircase ended. Alterations had taken place since my time but after several minutes walking up and down corridors we found the flight that led to the top floor.

The stairs were narrow and at their foot stood two guards. Both carried Russian AKM automatic rifles and their attitude showed that they were prepared to use them. Delaney casually slipped his rifle from his shoulder and leaned it against the wall. I quickly did the same, sensing the immediate lessening of tension. Delaney moved forward with his stolen identification papers in his hand and I followed. As he reached a position where one of the two men was blinded by the other he brought the papers nearer to his chest and using them as cover slid the pistol from beneath his jacket and rammed it hard into the man's stomach. The sudden exhalation of breath warned the second man that something was amiss but before he had time to move I stepped forward bringing out my pistol and slammed it against his temple.

Pushing the first man ahead of him Delaney went on up the stairs as I dragged the unconscious sentry by the heels through the nearest door into what appeared to be a kitchen. I flung our rifles after him and then, picking up the two AKM's, I hurried after Delaney and, seizing hold of the guard's sleeve, I asked him where the prisoner Altmann was held. He looked at me impassively. Both Delaney and I knew that whatever happened from that moment on we had a fight on our hands and that the need for furtiveness had ended.

We both started yelling Altmann's name. In the silence that followed I could hear my own breathing and heartbeat, neither sounding particularly relaxed. Suddenly we heard an answer, first in German and then in English. The voice came from a door a few paces down the corridor. Already other voices were raised and I heard feet pounding along a passage to my right. I reached the door and hopefully tried the handle. It was locked. "Stand away from the door," I shouted. "Turn your back and keep to the side." I hoped Altmann's English was sufficient to understand the words and with barely a pause I shot out the lock with three shots from the Beretta and kicked open the door. The man in the room turned slowly and looked at me, a strange expression on his face.

"Herr Altmann?"

"Yes."

"Your first name?"

"Gerhard Franz." I grinned with relief.

"I think we had better get out of here," I told him.

Chapter Six

I shoved the pistol back under my jacket and threw one of the AKM's to Delaney. By then the noise from all sides and particularly from below had increased. Delaney seemed quite relaxed as he headed back towards the staircase, pushing the guard in front of him. They went down the stairs to the next floor. With Altmann in front of me, I followed. I felt vulnerable and decided to do something about it. I called down to Delaney.

"We need another hostage fast, preferably someone with rank." Delaney half turned his head and nodded. At that moment the guard reached the third floor landing and moved suddenly to his left. Delaney was too quick for him and hit the man hard in the soft flesh over the kidneys. Delaney waved me down and propelling Altmann ahead of me I joined him. The guard looked slightly ill but not badly hurt and he had lost his enthusiasm for any further escape attempt. Motioning to me to keep the guard covered Delaney moved quickly down the corridor opening doors with a kick. The first was the kitchen door where I had dragged the unconscious guard. He was still lying where I had left him and there was no sign that he had moved. Delaney opened the next door and the next. He had broken the catches and strained the hinges on three more doors before he found what he wanted.

From my position I could not see what he had found but he reached forward and pulled a young woman into the corridor. He pushed her along towards me. She was about twenty and her dark, sultrily pretty face was filled with fear. I pushed down a momentary feeling of sympathy and walked quickly towards the head of the staircase. At least twenty men were positioned along the landing and down the stairs to the next level. Standing casually against the handrail at the staircase head was a slightly built exceptionally dark-skinned man in the uniform of a Major. I pushed the guard ahead of me and went close up to the officer.

"We are going out," I said hoping that my Arabic would stand its most important test so far. "No one has been killed. Co-operate and we can keep it that way. If you don't I have no doubt you will kill us in time but before then several of your men will die, starting with this one, then you and the girl." The Major stared back at me his face expressionless. His eyes flickered over the uniform I wore. For a second they lingered on the bullet hole in the breast but he decided not to press the point.

"You give me little choice," he said, his impeccable English showing what he thought of my Arabic. "Very well you can pass, not one of my men is going to die for that." He nodded dismissively at Altmann.

"Good," with relief I reverted to English, "but we'll have one change. You in place of him." I pushed the guard a pace forward. The Major was silent for a moment.

"Very well," he answered and slowly removed his revolver from the holster on his belt and gently laid the weapon on the floor. He came forward and stood in front of me. I pushed the guard further away and rested the muzzle of the AKM against the Major's chest.

"Now let's all be very careful," I said quietly, "when you speak, speak slowly and don't use dialect. Keep it simple. If you say anything I don't understand I'll kill you." The Major looked at me. I don't know what he saw in my eyes, fear probably, but he did not hesitate. He turned and ordered his men away from the head of the stairs. Those on the stairs were told to move down to the floor below. Slowly we began to descend the staircase. The events of the past few minutes had obviously been relayed ahead and as we reached first floor level I saw only one man and he was wearing the uniform of a Brigadier. I dropped my eyes to his revolver holster. It was empty. I looked up again and almost missed the merest nod that passed between the Brigadier and the Major. It could have been simply approval of the action the Major was taking or it could have been an indication that some standard emergency procedure was in operation. I decided not to take any chances. I reverted to

Arabic and called to the Brigadier.

"In case you have any doubts, we intend leaving here with this man," I gestured towards Altmann. "If any attempt is made to stop us we will kill him and we will kill the girl." The Brigadier's head jerked up at my last words. Obviously the message he had received had not mentioned the woman. Delaney who was at the rear pushed forward, impatient at the delay. He brought the girl with him and the sight of her brought a pronounced reaction from the Brigadier, then he recovered his poise and nodded.

"Wait. I will telephone. You will be permitted to leave the building and I will see to it that you have safe passage to . . . . . . where? The airport?"

"No, we have a vehicle and we will leave by road. We do want food and water, enough for all of us for five days." The Brigadier disappeared through a door and I heard him speaking on the telephone. I kept one ear cocked towards the doorway but he said nothing that made me any more worried than I was already. The Brigadier finished speaking and slowly and carefully we moved on down to the ground floor. I could feel the sweat pouring down my back. In minutes the Major led us out through the main doors and across the street that had been completely cleared of people and traffic. The Major stopped and I moved closer to him and pressed the muzzle of the AKM into his back. I pushed him forward and we walked quickly and warily towards the street where we had left the Gypsy. It was still there and I nudged the Major into the front passenger seat. Delaney made the girl sit on the Major's lap and then climbed into the back seat. He rested the gun muzzle on the back of the front seat just pressing against the Major's back and waited for me to open the bonnet, remove the spare rifle and refit the rotor arm. Surprisingly Altmann was still standing in the road and I told him to climb in beside Delaney.

I was about to hand him the rifle when Delaney said sharply, "No. Throw it away." I looked at Altmann but the grey haired German merely shrugged. There was no doubt about the expression he had on his face – bewilderment mixed with a little fear. Obviously, he did not know what was going on or why. He was getting out of prison, however, and for the moment that seemed to be enough for him.

I checked my watch, it was just after eight and already dark. It was hard to believe that all that had happened had been compressed into five hours. I threw the rifle onto the pavement and climbed into the driving seat. I started the engine and drove slowly back to the prison gates. The food and water we had requested was piled in boxes and between us Altmann and I stowed them in any odd corner of the truck that was not already occupied. I started the engine again and in a few minutes we were on Al Raschid Street, the main road through the centre of the city. There the traffic was flowing quickly and I had my hands full threading my way through fast moving, mainly American, cars that were being driven by maniacs whose principal technique was to keep their horns sounding in a constant deafening racket. It was over half an hour before we cleared the city and were heading south on the main road to Hillah.

We were about forty miles out of the city when the Gypsy lurched, the steering wheel twisting in my hands. One of the front tyres had blown out and I braked quickly as I pulled the vehicle onto the right hand shoulder. The jack and wheelbrace were pushed under the front passenger seat and I dragged them out from behind the legs of the Major and the woman. I released the spare wheel that was clamped to the bonnet and then climbed back into the driving seat to manoeuver the Gypsy until the offside wheel, the one with the blow-out, was firm on the edge of the road surface.

"Give me a hand," I said to Altmann as I climbed out again and started to ease the wheel nuts. Altmann climbed down and pushed the jack into place. As I finished loosening the nuts Altmann was ready and he slotted the jack lever into place and started lifting the Gypsy. I finished spinning off the wheel nuts. That done I pulled the wheel free as Altmann continued raising the body the few inches more needed to allow the inflated tyre to clear the ground. The new wheel was fitted, the body lowered and the wheel nuts tightened within a few minutes. The pits at Silverstone would have been proud of us. I started to gather the pieces of equipment together but Altmann stopped me.

"Why bother?" he said, "you can't change it again." He was right and although we were not in a hurry, standing exposed by the roadside was not comfortable. I waved Altmann into the back seat of the Gypsy. I hurried round and climbed back into the driving seat and before everyone was settled into place I engaged gear and let the clutch in with a bang. We shot away spraying sand behind us as I pushed the jeep to over seventy miles an hour, a speed for which the road surface was not really suitable.

Half an hour later I could make out rooftops on the left hand side of the road. I slowed down and, as we came up to the bridge over the river, I checked carefully the amount of river traffic faintly visible in the light of the few lamps illuminating the wharf. Luckily there was very little, a few barges and river boats moored on the side that had the concrete wharf and nothing moored against the opposite bank. That gave Potter plenty of room for landing and was the first of the two reasons for this preliminary reconnaissance, the second was to make certain that we could get to the Cessna without having to swim for it. I didn't know if Altmann could swim but I certainly couldn't and I had no intention of being left behind.

Fortunately there seemed to be no problem, several small rowing boats and even one or two coracles were tied up amongst the bigger boats and there was every reason to expect that at least one of them would be there the following evening when we would need it. I was reasonably certain that the Brigadier at the prison would know where we were and not wanting to risk giving him a clue to our plans by showing too much interest in the river, I picked up speed again.

I drove on for about ten more miles before I switched off the headlamps as I saw a cluster of lights travelling towards us. I braked and as the vehicles passed I swung the Gypsy round and followed the last truck in the line, with my lights still off. I stayed in the convoy as it went past Hillah and back along the road towards Baghdad. After a few more miles I saw the signpost I was looking for and turned left off the main road. The condition of the narrow side road was very bad and we were jolted about as I drove the

Gypsy carefully up the slight gradient. Minutes later we arrived and I switched off the engine. The silence was so complete it was like pressure on the nerves.

"Welcome," I said, "to Babylon."

No one seemed very impressed. Still holding the AKM I moved away from the Gypsy aware that the others were also climbing down. Delaney, I knew, would have the Major and the girl under careful watch and I did not expect trouble from Altmann. I wanted to check that we were as alone as I expected and wanted us to be. I sensed rather than saw Altmann come up beside me and I had half turned to speak before I realised that he was swinging something through the air. I threw myself sideways taking the blow on my shoulder. That was better than my head but the sudden extreme pain almost made me lose consciousness. I went to my knees, then gathering myself for a moment, I swung the rifle catching Altmann in the side just below his rib cage. He fell and for a moment we were both on our knees, our eyes only inches apart. I recovered first. I slipped the safety on the AKM and pushed the muzzle hard into his throat, he gagged and then let drop the object he had used to attack me. It was the jack handle. That accounted for his earlier efficiency. I picked up the steel bar and flung it into the darkness then I pulled Altmann to his feet and pushed him over to where Delaney stood.

"We'll have to tie them all up," Delaney said. "The girl and the Major together, keep Altmann apart." I used the Major's tie and belt to secure him to the girl. I could find nothing with which to tie Altmann's hands and I finally tore strips from his own shirt. Once finished I pushed the three towards the Gypsy and helped them make themselves as comfortable as possible. That done I turned to Delaney.

"Well?" He looked at me and then looked up at the sky.

"What about an aerial search? If someone comes over here they will see us in the morning."

"There is cover not far from here. What's going on? I guessed from the start that it wasn't all as you told me. That's fair enough I suppose. But when the man I'm risking my life to rescue tries to beat my brains out, I draw the line. Who is Altmann and . . . . . .?"

"Wait a minute," he interrupted me. "Look, you're right. There is more in this than we told you. It's Potter's deal and it's up to him to explain it all to you if he wants to. As for Altmann, Potter needs him for the deal we're working on. He is vital. Neither of us have met him before. He was in prison for some arms smuggling he had been doing with the Kurds and one or two other things besides. He's under sentence of death."

"So he should be pleased to get out."

"Maybe. Maybe he prefers to try it alone. After all he doesn't know about the aircraft. He thinks we're going out by road."

"And you're not going to tell me what this is all about?"

"No."

"Okay, I'll wait for Potter to tell me, but remember, I'm armed as well and if you try anything with me you're just as likely to end up dead as I am. And if trouble does start, I'll see to it that Altmann dies first, then whatever it is you want him for, will end right there." There seemed no point in any further discussion and I turned away. Any thought of taking turns to keep watch had gone from my mind. Both of us would stay awake through the night, watching each other at least as carefully as the three tied in the jeep.

As the night wore on I sensed that Delaney had relaxed. Logic must have told him that I was the last man he should argue with. Without me he would be in even more trouble. There was no way he could guard the hostages and Altmann and rendezvous with Potter. I relaxed as well but staying awake still seemed like a good idea. The following day which had to be spent in that same place would be time enough to discuss things cooly with Delaney and arrive at a workable truce which would allow us both to sleep without fear of attack.

The silence was no longer as total as it had seemed immediately after switching off the engine and I could hear tiny croaking noises from some kind of animal or insect as well as the faint murmur of the breeze that blew softly through the passages and along the walls of the ancient city. It should have been peaceful, but it wasn't; instead it filled me with an almost tangible sense of dread.

Chapter Seven

An hour before dawn I cautiously moved the Gypsy. I couldn't risk using the lights and at the same time I had to avoid putting a wheel into a deep crevice. The tumbled-down wall I remembered had the remains of an arch which gave sufficient cover for anyone trying to spot us from the air. It would also give us much needed cover from the sun which would soon be rising. Everyone was awake. Nobody spoke. I sat far enough away to avoid having to look at, or talk to anyone but close enough to get under cover if the need arose. I needed sleep and I needed a clear head. I wasn't likely to get either.

Self-analysis is something I have always avoided but I indulged myself then. Letting myself be talked into the trip to Eymoutiers was easily explained. No apparent risk for a good return. But was no risk apparent? Right from the start I hadn't trusted Potter, but I had gone along with the plan anyway. Then the set-up in France and the black-mail to get me where I was. The French police were not idiots and I should have dug in my heels when I still thought that was who I was involved with. But I didn't. And then I had seen Christine on the jetty at Kyrenia. Right then I should have called a halt. Even at that late stage I could have done so if I had tried. But I didn't try. It all came down to one thing in the end. As I had already accepted, Potter had found my price. Added to that I was curious, very curious to know what Potter and Delaney were up to and where Christine and Erich von Stroheim fitted in to it all. And Altmann.

Altmann. I looked across at him in the brightening light. About fifty, I guessed, plump, grey-haired and if a one-word definition was needed, innocuous. Potter and Delaney had to want him badly. After all, it wasn't just my life they were risking, it was theirs too. Whatever it was Altmann had, it had to be big.

I walked over to Delaney and he grinned tightly as I reached him.

"You can relax," he said, "I know as well as you do that I need you to get out of this place and you know that if you show up at the river without me Potter will leave you behind. So we call a truce. Okay?"

I wondered if he was right, my guess was that if I turned up at the river without Delaney, but with Altmann, then Potter wouldn't be very bothered about the loss of his partner. I kept my thought to myself.

"There doesn't seem to be much choice but remember, I'm not taking any chances." I helped our prisoners, by then I was classing Altmann as a captive, out of the vehicle and, taking care to keep Altmann between me and Delaney, I untied their hands and then helped the Major and the girl back into the Gypsy and into a more comfortable position.

I opened one of the boxes the Brigadier had supplied. The food looked decidedly unappetising, chupattis and some reddish coloured goo that looked like cold stew. I handed round the dry platelike cakes and led the way by scooping up some of the mixture and eating. Surprisingly enough the taste was not all that bad. It was highly spiced and apparently more vegetable than meat but it was edible and we were all very hungry. Even the girl, who had done nothing but look frightened to death, attacked the food with some enthusiasm. As I ate I checked through the other boxes. One held water bottles the others all held the same food, chup-pattis and red stew. I hoped our plans would not go astray. More than one day on that diet and my stomach would surrender even if the rest of me wanted to fight on. I handed round one water bottle and we emptied it between us.

I was putting the boxes back into the Gypsy when the visitor arrived. I had completely forgotten the guides to the ruined city of Babylon. Half a dozen semi-official individuals who lived amongst the ruins and eked a precarious and at times non-existant living from tourists who came to see the ruins. The sight of five potential customers was too much for that one. He let out a welcoming yell and I leaped to my feet reaching for the automatic rifle that lay close to my hand. Delaney did the same and we stared at the guide as he advanced smiling delightedly and already breaking into his patter.

I heard a scrambling sound behind me and turned to see the Major disappearing round the corner of a crumbling wall. Altmann and girl had not moved and I was past them and after the Major before Delaney reacted. He was not likely to stray far from Altmann and he would take care of the old man, hopefully without violence.

I reached the wall and went round it without pausing. I didn't expect the Major to attempt to tackle me as I thought he would be too intent on getting away and revealing our position. If I had stopped to reason I might have known better but I didn't. I ran round the corner without breaking my stride and the rock the Major threw hit me squarely in the chest. I went over backwards the breath knocked out of me but I kept hold of the AKM and that left me with an edge. The Major followed the rock in a low dive that was meant to pin me to the ground but I avoided him by rolling sideways a half turn and then as he landed on the hard ground beside me I rolled back bringing the sharp cornered metal butt of the rifle down into the small of his back. I started to get to my feet and for the second time in as many minutes misjudged my opponent. His legs wrapped round mine and I went crashing down again, this time to land on my face. Again I held onto the weapon and I came off the ground fast, not giving him a chance to get to his feet, but he pulled the oldest trick in the book and it worked perfectly. He scooped up a handful of sand and threw it into my eyes. By the time I had cleared them, he had gone.

I scrambled over the rocks and then stopped, listening. After a moment I heard him away to my right and I headed in the direction of the sound but with considerably more caution than I had shown before. He must have been hurt by the blow in the back for he was making a lot of noise. I knew that it could have been a trick but I decided to take a chance. I had only the vaguest memory of the layout of the ruins but I felt certain that he would try to get down to the lower level away from the possibility of presenting me with an easy target for, as far as he knew, I was likely to start shooting. He was probably heading for one of the long staircases that ran down the outside of several of the high walls. I ran through the ruins keeping well clear of the area I thought he was in and went round in a circle that brought me to the top of a wall looking down into one of the old thoroughfares. The roadway was almost two storeys below where I stood. It was reached by a staircase that ran down the wall opposite to where I waited. The stairs were about four feet wide and open on the outer edge. Along the wall that made the inner edge of the stairs were bas-reliefs of ancient gods. If they thought anything of what was going on in their domain, they kept it to themselves. I waited quietly, the Major was still making a lot of noise and after a moment he appeared at the head of the stairway. I let him get halfway down before I spoke.

"That's far enough Major. Stand quite still." He stopped and looked up at me. He glanced up and down the stairway and accepted the impossibility of his situation with a shrug. I walked carefully along the top of the wall and around the end of the stairwell and clambered over the piles of excavated sand and earth until I reached the head of the stairs.

"Start back up. Move slowly." He did as he was told and I waited until he climbed wearily to stand before me. We looked at each other.

"Why?" he asked. "Why all this for a man like that? What has he got that you want so badly? He is just as arms dealer. He has no political preferences; he deals with whoever pays his price. We would have no quarrel with him if he had not entered the country at our invitation, only to use the visit as a means of trying to deal with the Kurds. He can't be that important. Why go to all this trouble?"

"No questions Major. Just do as you're told from now on and no one will get hurt. We will be out of your country very soon and then you can forget all about us." We started back towards the others. Then I remembered something and I stopped him. "The girl. Your Brigadier reacted strongly when he saw we had her. Who is she?" He looked at me in silence. Clearly he was weighing the pros and cons of lying or speaking the truth. When he answered he had obviously decided on the truth.

"She's his daughter. She works as a secretary in the interrogation department." I thought about that for a moment. The advantage was obvious, we were safe just so long as we had her. Equally obviously, if we lost her we would get very little in the way of sympathetic treatment. I decided to see that she was treated as well as possible in the circumstances – which meant not telling Delaney. He was sufficiently unpredictable to use that kind of knowledge to nobody's benefit.

When we got back to the others there was no sign that Delaney had had any trouble. Altmann and the girl were exactly where they had been and the old man was sitting crouched against the radiator of the Gypsy. Delaney glanced at the Major and me.

"Well?"

"No problem, no one else was about." I went on to tell him who the old man was and why he was there. He grunted when I had finished but he didn't say anything. I was beginning to react to the fight and my chest was aching where the Major's rock had found it's mark. "We both need sleep," I ended "and soon."

"Agreed, tie them up again. The Major and the girl together in the jeep. Tie the old guy to the back. Altmann, tie him to the steering wheel and we'd better take shifts, short ones, say two hours each. That way we're less likely to fall asleep."

After securing the four prisoners I took the first sleeping turn although I didn't manage to sleep even though by then I was very tired. During the remainder of the day I did manage a few minutes sleep in some of my off-watch periods but I was far from rested when at four o'clock in the afternoon we were ready to move off. With Delaney keeping a careful watch I released Altmann and the guide. I left the Major and the girl tied together in the back seat of the Gypsy.

"What about the old man?" I asked. "Do we leave him here or take him with us?"

"Leave him; he can't do us much harm. He doesn't know where we are heading, or why and, by the time he gets to an official, we should be on our way home. Anyway the chances are he won't bother to report what has happened."

Delaney was probably right and I improved the chances of the old man not reporting us by handing him a bundle of notes; more than he would normally make in six months. He seemed astonished at the way things had turned out for him and he scuttled off over the ruins in the opposite direction to the main road.

I walked over to the Gypsy and tried to smile reassuringly at the girl who looked close to breaking point. I had difficulty in arranging my face muscles into the right shape and the result seemed to do nothing to remove her fears. Delaney climbed into the back of the Gypsy with the Major and the girl, the muzzle of the AKM as steady as ever and close to the Major's side. I thought for a moment and then told Altmann to get behind the wheel. I climbed in and handed him the keys. The German seemed resigned to his enforced escape.

"Take it steadily and do precisely as you are told," I told him. He started the engine and looked enquiringly at me. I nodded and we moved off slowly, back down the track leading to the main road where I told Altmann to turn right and soon we were motoring gently down the road towards Hillah.

It was about ten minutes to five when we reached the edge of the little town. I kept my eyes on the far side of the road until I could make out the masts of the river boats in the already fading light.

"Slow down," I told Altmann. "Turn left here, slowly now." As we left the road the Gypsy's headlights swept across the concrete wharf.

"Stop here," I ordered. Before the vehicle had stopped I jumped down and using the headlights to guide me I ran along the edge of the wharf, peering down into the river until I found what we wanted; a small rowing boat moored at the foot of an iron ladder built into the wall. I turned and waved to Delaney and as I did so I heard the sound of an aeroplane engine. I couldn't identify the sound but I had no doubt that it was the Cessna. Behind me I heard a yell and a scuffle. I sprinted back and passed Delaney who was hurrying Altmann ahead of him.

"What happened?"

"The Major decided to be a hero," he told me. When I reached the jeep, the Major was slumped unconscious on the back seat.

"It's all over now," I reassured the girl as I reached in and started flashing the headlights downriver towards the now rapidly approaching aircraft.

Suddenly a beam of light appeared in the sky as Potter switched on his landing lights. As the engine note changed I left the Gypsy and ran back to the rowing boat. I reached the top of the ladder just as Delaney, who had put Altmann in the boat first, stepped into the small craft. I threw the AKM into the river and with the Beretta in my right hand I half climbed, half slid down the ladder. As soon as I was in the boat Delaney picked up one oar and with Altmann at the other they began to push away from the side as I hastily released the mooring rope from the gunwhale. In the excitement I had lost track of the aircraft but looking round I saw it a hundred yards up river, Potter had already landed and was taxi-ing back towards us. The landing lights were out and a small hand spotlight, operated from the cockpit, arced across the water. In seconds it found us and the Cessna turned and moved closer. I was vaguely aware of shouting from the river bank but I ignored the sounds. No one was likely to start shooting, not without knowing who was on the river. The Major would still be unconscious and the girl was not likely to be making much sense to anyone who found her.

The Cessna had stopped moving and Delaney took the oar from Altmann and manoeuvered the little boat alongside. The cargo door in the port side had been opened and I made sure I was the first to scramble aboard. I turned and helped Altmann in. Delaney followed, swinging himself up out of the boat with ease. As soon as he was on board, I turned away leaving him to shut the door. I moved to the seat next to Altmann and looked at Potter who was watching us a broad grin on his face.

"Well done chaps, now I think we had better get out of here before our presence becomes offensive to someone." Delaney pushed past and crowded into the seat beside Potter. The engine noise increased as Potter turned on the power and in moments the little float-plane was roaring along the river its lights blazing once more. I felt my stomach lurch once and then we were airborne. I sat back in my seat and slowly relaxed. I realised I still held the pistol and as I pushed the weapon under my shirt I was conscious that beside me the German also relaxed.

Potter took the Cessna up to about one thousand feet. At that altitude the evening sky seemed brighter and I could see the town of Hillah clearly below us. We had been airborne for ten minutes when Potter put the nose down and took us to a frighteningly low altitude. He banked the Cessna and we went into a steep turn that set us going back the way we had flown into Iraq – northwest. The Cessna descended further and I decided that three hours of near suicidal low level flying was more than my nerves could stand. I closed my eyes and forced my mind to go blank hoping that sleep would come. Surprisingly enough it did, although the noise made real rest impossible.

Chapter Eight

I was brought sharply awake when the Cessna lurched sideways as Potter made a turn that almost threw me from my seat; only the cramped conditions kept me in place. I looked at the luminous face of my watch. We had been airborne from Hillah for just over two hours. I tried to picture the maps Potter and I had pored over during the planning stage. Assuming that Potter had been holding normal cruising speed we had crossed the border and were in Syrian air space. The Cessna went into another sudden turn that left my stomach somewhere behind us.

"What's going on?" I yelled at Potter. He took no notice of me and it was Delaney who leaned back and told me what was happening.

"There's another plane out there. As far as we can see it's a jet fighter."

I peered out into the night, the moon was completely covered and visibility was almost nil. I felt Altmann clutch at my sleeve and I turned to look out of the window on his side.

Above us about half a mile away were the navigation lights of an aircraft. I could see that ours were off. Potter was obviously keeping the other pilot guessing. I assumed that in the absence of moonlight he had been using the powerful landing lights to follow the pipeline and that by chance a pilot on a night flight had spotted us and come down to investigate. I had not realised that being in such a slow speed aircraft would give us an important advantage. The jet was probably travelling more than five times as fast as we were and the differential gave us a chance. The navigation lights above our port wing had drawn well ahead and watching carefully I saw a change in their configuration. The jet had changed course and was flying across our path. It was doubtful if he could see us and was probably making an exploratory sweep.

Fortunately, he appeared to be maintaining an altitude of about fifteen hundred feet and that kept him well above us. Potter had settled the Cessna onto a steady course and I didn't like to think how close to the ground we were. Potter must have been mind reading.

"We're a little too close to the ground for comfort, without the lights I can't risk staying down here." I reached forward and yelled in his ear.

"We can't hang about here either. He must have radiod back to his base by now and they will be looking for us on radar even if they don't send others up after us." Potter nodded, the outline of his head fringed by the greenish glow from the instrument panel. He lifted the nose of the Cessna and we began to climb. At the same instant there was a break in the clouds and the moon shone through and the bright yellow of the Cessna must have made us as easy to spot as if we had been in a searchlight. The jet came down towards us from ahead and pulled terrifyingly close before breaking away leaving a trembling roar that reverberated through the cabin. Fortunately the pilot appeared to have used that pass as a means of seeing what, if not who, we were. The sight of a harmless little passenger plane must have been as much of a surprise to him as his presence was a threat to us.

"Did you see what it was?" Potter called to me.

"It looked like an old Lightning but it can't be one of those, they're obsolete."

"It might be a MIG 21. They look like a P1, at least in these conditions, and the Syrian Air Force has a squadron of them."

"Does it matter what it is? We're sunk anyway."

"You give up too easily Mr. Stanway." Potter was maintaining the climb and his voice was quite calm, almost casual.

"What can we do?"

"Our friend up there has a very fast machine and unless he is very good indeed he might find low level manoeuvering a bit tricky. With luck we can lead him into making a mistake."

"How for God's sake?" Potter did not bother to reply and concentrated on levelling the Cessna out at what I guessed was about three thousand feet. The moon was still showing through the clouds and I tried in vain to spot the fighter.

"All of you keep watch on the clouds," Potter called. "Forget the jet. As soon as you think the clouds are going to blot out the moon tell me. Give me as much warning as you can." We did as we were told. From my side of the cabin the moon was not visible but the jet was and I told Potter.

"What is he doing?"

"He's flying in the same direction as we are and he's overhauling us fast."

"Good. Keep watching him." We flew on for about two more minutes then Delaney shouted out to Potter that a cloud was about to obscure the moon. By then the jet was well ahead and about two thousand feet above us. Potter didn't need telling as the fighter was clearly visible through the windscreen. He reached forward and pressed a switch and all the lights came on, navigation lights and landing lights, in a sudden blaze. In the same instant he threw the Cessna into a tight port turn, put the nose down and we roared towards the ground.

"Watch him. Tell me where he is." I twisted round in my seat and in the few seconds before the clouds covered the moon I spotted the jet rolling over and starting to follow us down.

"He's following us. I can't see him now. Wait, yes I've got his lights. Christ he's coming fast."

"Hold on." Potter yelled and, as I turned to face forward, he hit a switch and all the lights went out, but not before I had caught a glimpse of the ground seemingly within a few feet of our nose. As the scene below us blacked out, Potter swung the Cessna into an apparently impossible starboard turn and simultaneously brought the nose up into a climb. The Cessna creaked and shuddered around us but somehow it stayed in one piece. By then I had lost track of the MIG even though less than twenty seconds had elapsed since I had turned away from it. Potter had obviously known precisely where it was and at that instant he hit the light switch again and all our lights came back on.

We were directly in the flightpath of the jet and we were very close to it, too close for the pilot to take time to think but not so close that he didn't have time to react instinctively. He banked the MIG to the left and those few precious split seconds were enough to save our lives. They were also the split seconds the pilot should have used to get out of his dive. He didn't and he had not realised or, in the excitement of the chase, he had forgotten how close he was to the ground.

The roar as he went past us was deafening and so was the explosion as he hit the ground seconds later. In the splash of flame I could see that the jet had landed on top of a pumping station on the pipeline and about half a minute later, before I had begun to grasp the enormity of what had already happened, the station went up in a roaring torrent of flame. The blast threw us about like a yellow leaf but Potter maintained the total control he had displayed throughout the flight and soon the flames, leaping to leave a glow in the night sky, were fading behind us. The panic and chaos the crash must have caused, gave us what we needed – time. We were less than one hour from the coastline and I sweated every minute of the journey until Potter announced that we were out of Syrian airspace and heading for Cyprus.

I began to relax for the first time for hours. Beside me Altmann turned his head very slightly and looked at me out of the corner of his eyes. Delaney and Potter were both looking straight ahead. When Altmann spoke I could barely hear his voice over the sound of the engine.

"Why have you taken me from there?" I decided that the opportunity to learn something more about the plump German was too good to miss. Without moving my head I answered keeping my voice pitched as low as possible.

"I'm just the hired hand. You tell me why they want you."

"I have never seen those men before in my life. Perhaps they have mistaken me for someone else. Perhaps they think that I am a different Altmann."

I shook my head.

"No. They haven't gone to all this trouble for the wrong

man. You are the one they want. If you don't know what they want we will have to wait until we arrive."

"Arrive where?"

"Cyprus."

"Why Cyprus?"

"It is the nearest place where a seaplane would not attract too much attention and still within range of the prison."

"Very well, I suppose we must wait." Altmann hesitated, "Your shoulder. . . . . . I am sorry, I was very alarmed and I feared for my life." He paused again, longer this time, then almost inaudibly he added, "I still do." I looked at him and then turned away quickly as Potter called out over his shouder.

"Not long now old boy." I was aware that the German beside me was looking hard at Potter. He turned his head slightly and whispered.

"The pilot, I think perhaps I have seen him before. What is his name?"

"Potter." The German shook his head.

"No I do not recall the name. Perhaps I am mistaken." Delaney moved in his seat and stretched his cramped muscles. He turned and looked back at me and then reached down beside his seat and put on a headset. Potter looked across, puzzled as Delaney motioned to him to do the same. When Potter had the set on Delaney started talking. There was no doubt that he was telling Potter of the events of the night before and what I knew and that I was no longer happy with the reasons I had been given for the escape. When Delaney finished his report Potter took off the headset and turned to me.

"Should be over St. Andreas soon," he called. "Not long after that we will be safe and sound." He smiled his usual smile. Delaney's report did not appear to have unsettled him in any way. I changed my position in my seat and as I did so I felt the Beretta dig into my ribs. I slipped a hand inside my shirt and moved the gun to a more comfortable position. The movement did not escape Altmann's attention and he looked at me and smiled conspiratorially. I found the man's misconception of my movements slightly irritating. Although I did not feel any more trust for Potter and

Delaney than I had from the beginning, I was by no means certain that I was ready to change my allegiance. After all, only Potter had offered me money.

Delaney clambered out of his seat and moved into one of the seats in front of Altmann and me. Laid out on them were neat bundles of clothing held in place by the seat belts.

"Time to change," Delaney announced. "When we land we want to look like tourists," he added for Altmann's benefit. I hesitated.

"We keep to the plan, all guns go into the sea as soon as we touch down," he said, and slipped his own pistol out, unloaded it, then reached forward and picked up the remaining AKM and did the same with that. He stuffed the bullets into the pockets of the clothes he was wearing and then struggled out of the dirty army uniform. He redressed in a sports shirt and slacks. Slowly I brought out the Beretta. Delaney and I looked at each other. "As soon as we are ashore Potter will tell you the full story and you will be in for a full share when Altmann tells us what we want to know."

"Tell you what," interrupted Altmann, "there is nothing I can tell you. What is it you want?" Delaney looked at the man, his expression hard and emotionless.

"We want to know where you hid the gold of course." Altmann drew in his breath harshly. I looked at him, then turned to Delaney, but he was already back in his seat. I started to change my clothes. When I had finished I nudged the German who slowly began to change into the clothes Potter had provided.

The Cessna banked gently to port and as the wingtip dipped I could see the lights of the Cape of St. Andreas glinting below. Potter began a long descent and about thirty minutes later we bounced onto the sea in a rush of white spray. Potter had put the floatplane down well out to sea and as he turned inshore I could see the lights of Kyrenia about threequarters of a mile away. As we taxied slowly inshore Delaney came back and we threw the weighted uniforms through the door. I took care to handle the bundle myself so that Delaney would not know that it did not weigh quite as much as it should have done. Altmann sat motionless staring out of the window. When the Cessna was alongside the mooring buoy Potter switched off the engine and turned round grinning happily.

"Well that's that. I think a drink, a shower and a meal and then a long talk." The last part of his remark was directed at Altmann who looked up at Potter with the same expression I had seen earlier. He nodded slowly and Potter and Delaney looked at each other smiling.

I had to wait another hour before my curiosity was satisfied. I had the shower and the meal that Potter had recommended but I missed out the drink. When I had dressed again I slipped out of the hotel and walked down to the jetty. I took the rowing boat we had used to come ashore and went out to the Cessna. I climbed on board and pushed my hand down the back of the seat I had been using. I pulled out the Beretta and slipped it into the waistband of my trousers. I felt a twinge of unrealistic conscience at my deceit but that was quickly removed by the thought that the others, Delaney certainly, would have a weapon of some kind. I rowed back to the jetty and walked slowly up towards the hotel, a fierce excitement starting to grip at my stomach. All because of one word Delaney had used. Gold.

When I walked into Potter's room Delaney looked the same as he had at our first meeting, as if the events of the preceding days had been nothing more strenuous than a sightseeing tour. Potter sat in an armchair languidly finishing a small scotch. I refused a drink and looked at Altmann who appeared to have recovered a little. I looked enquiringly at Potter who accepted the look as an invitation for an explanation.

"First old boy, my apologies. Should have given you the whole story but we didn't know how far we could trust you." He paused, finished his drink, and held up the glass for Delaney to replenish it. A fresh drink in his hand, he continued. "During the last ten years or so I have been collecting facts, snippets here, snippets there, half truths and speculations all relating to certain events that involved Mr. Altmann many years ago. But of Mr. Altmann himself there was no sign until he was arrested in Iraq and a photograph of him appeared in a newspaper. The death sentence passed on him was a blow and I resolved to get him out. Mr. Delaney was already in my employ but for that particular job it was obvious that someone with specialist knowledge was needed. That was you." I didn't need telling how he had found out about me. My ex-wife had obviously contributed that information.

"Very interesting," I told him, "but you still haven't told me why."

"Ah yes, the reason why." He paused and for an instant I thought it was for effect but when he started to speak again the tone of his voice spoke of something else, something that affected him deeply and that he had lived with for a very long time. "You have probably heard about the theft from Germany of gold bullion at the end of the war. A team of American and German military personnel and a few German civilians removed several million pounds worth from the Federal reserve vaults. Nothing has been seen of it since. Not a trace. A beautiful job." Potter went on half to himself. "Millions of pounds worth at 1945 prices. The value today would be incalculable." The three of us were looking at Altmann. The German stared into his glass. I glanced at the others. In Delaney's face I could see a mixture of greed and admiration. I could not identify the expression on Potter's face but whatever it concealed I felt a slight stirring of unease. Potter caught my eyes on him and all expression vanished and the bland Potter returned to the surface.

"I think it is time we heard from Mr. Altmann," Potter said turning to the German. "Perhaps you would care to tell us what happened, from the beginning."

Altmann looked at us each in turn and after a moment he began to speak quietly. Apart from his voice there was silence in the room. As he spoke I could picture the scene being described even though it was a place I had never seen in a land I had never visited. The Klausenkopf mountains in Bavaria. Bavaria in the summer of 1945.

Chapter Nine

Bavaria in the summertime was beautiful but Altmann had had no time to admire the scenery as he had wrestled with the steering wheel of the heavy truck. The fading light, coupled with the dust raised by the wheels of the lorry he was following had made visibility bad and he had concentrated all his attention on his driving. From time to time he had risked a hasty sideways glance at the man sitting beside him. Sergeant Böhm was a thin, dark, quick-moving man. Altmann had known him by sight but until that day he had not been in his company. And now suddenly he was the Sergeant's partner in a crime, an incomprehensibly massive theft. And worse, he was a partner, however unwilling, in murder. As he drove he had tried to marshal his jumbled thoughts into order. Thoughts that had raced with excitement, fear and greed.

He had been a fighting soldier in an army he had once believed invincible. That this army was not invincible had been apparent for many long months and he had known that they were plunging towards defeat in the closing trap between the advancing American, British and Russian armies. Then, inexplicably at first, he had been posted to a quiet corner of Bavaria. Inexplicable, that is, until he had found out what it was he was there to do. He had joined the detachment that guarded the bullion reserves of the almost defeated nation. The vaults that had held the gold had been built deep into the side of a mountain in the Klausenkopf range and the responsibility had been awesome until he had realised that while he knew who to guard against, there was no longer anyone to guard it for.

The war had ended and the Americans had come and suddenly he was a prisoner and just as suddenly he was free again. The senior American officer, a Colonel, had taken only minutes to assess what he had stumbled upon and he had taken even less time to decide what to do about it.

He had decided to steal the gold. But he had needed help – American help, as he had to trust someone, and German help, as he had to have local knowledge. This was where he had made his mistake. He had picked Altmann and a dull slow private called Schneider and Böhm and another man Altmann had never seen. He was tall and thin, a sandy featureless man who had always worn sunglasses and who had never spoken to anyone but Böhm, and then only in whispers. Böhm had called him Max and what they had whispered about had been suddenly made apparent when all the gold bullion had been packed into empty ammunition boxes and loaded onto two heavy trucks. The American Colonel had been distracted by Max suddenly making a move as if to run for it. He had turned his back on Böhm, and the Sergeant had thrown himself at the American. Altmann had seen a knife flash brightly in the sunlight and then Böhm and Max were armed, Böhm with the American's revolver and Max with his Johnson light machine gun. In seconds the remaining Americans were dead and Altmann and Schneider were at the wheels of the two trucks. With Max watching them carefully they had waited until Böhm had dragged the bodies into the Colonel's jeep. Then Max had climbed in beside Schneider and Böhm beside Altmann. They were moving away when the explosion came. In his mirror Altmann had seen the jeep become a funeral pyre and then it had gone from sight as they rounded a bend in the road.

Slowly and deviously over the next few days they had driven down into Italy. Before firing the jeep Böhm had taken two uniforms from the dead Americans. He had worn one and Max the other but it had not mattered. No one had been interested in them for the end of hostilities had served only to aggravate problems of food and refugees, the sick and the dying. They had eaten infrequently, risking buying bread, sausage and wine only when there were no soldiers about, and they had refuelled twice at American army motor compounds where Max had done the talking in what had sounded to Altmann's ears like American-accented English.

He had estimated that they had stolen over twelve thousand kilogrammes of gold, an incalculable fortune. And all to be shared between four. If the killing had ended. That was what had been uppermost in his mind as they had travelled south-west from Parma. Would he and Schneider end as the Americans had ended or were they still needed? Twice he had a chance to run away and twice he had resisted the impulse to take it. He knew he had to stay and take that chance. Gold fever had overtaken him.

Late in the afternoon of the third day the leading truck had slowed suddenly and had turned off the road they were on, plunging into a lightly wooded area. Laboriously they had driven the vehicles through the narrow gaps between the trees until they were out of sight of anyone on the road. They had then switched off the engines.

The sudden silence after the constant racket of the past hours had dinned on Altmann's ears as he had climbed from the cab. The four men had stood silently looking at one another and Altmann had felt a sudden tug of fear but slowly Böhm had started to grin and soon all four were laughing at the release of tension. Altmann had been tired and had wanted to sleep but the others had seemed alert and as he had already estimated that all of them were ten years older than himself he had said nothing. Böhm and Max had walked away and had sat down against the bole of a tree where they had started to talk in undertones. Altmann and Schneider had collected the remains of the food and drink from the trucks and by the time they had done that Böhm and Max had finished their conference and Böhm quickly outlined their plans for the next few hours. They were a few kilometres outside the small coastal town of La Spezia. They would wait where they were until dusk when two of them would go down through the town to the village of Portovenere, where they hoped they would find a boat big enough to carry the bullion. If necessary they would use more than one boat and if they failed to find anything that was suitable they would move further on down the coast until they found what they needed. Whatever happened, nothing that could provide a lead to the direction they had taken would be left behind. Settling down on the hard ground they had eaten their remaining food, finished the wine and then they had dozed until daylight had started to fade.

Max and Schneider were the guards and Böhm and Altmann had taken off their jackets and, dressed only in boots, trousers and shirts, they had made their way back along the track they had followed in the trucks until they reached the roadside. Staying in the trees they had followed the road down to the town. No one had been about and they had hurried through the dark streets and on to Portovenere. About twenty small boats were tied up in the tiny harbour but Böhm had hurried along with barely a glance in their direction. Altmann had seen other, bigger boats tied up half way along the mole that jutted into the still water. They had reached them and Böhm had gone on board each in turn, but had climbed off the last of the boats and had stood shaking his head slowly. Out to sea Altmann had made out a dark shape some distance outside the harbour entrance. He had told Böhm and in a few minutes they were in a rowing boat pulling quietly out towards the shape. It had taken ten minutes before they had been close enough to identify the vessel as an American Army tank landing-craft. Bohm's teeth had gleamed whitely in the dim light from the cloud-obscured moon. Their luck was still holding. On board the landing-craft Böhm had checked the fuel tanks and the ignition system. He had told Altmann there was adequate fuel for their needs and the ignition system obviously held no problems for him. The craft had been moored to a buoy and they had released it and secured the rope to the rowing boat. They had pulled slowly towards the shoreline beyond the harbour until they were close into the sandy beach. It had taken them some time to find a stretch where the sand sloped steeply enough to allow the landing craft to be brought in later. When Böhm was satisfied they were in a suitable place they had dragged the rowing boat high up on the beach and after ensuring the landing-craft was secure as it rode gently on the still water they had hurried back towards the houses of the little village. Silently, the two men had moved back along the road to La Spezia and then on through the woods to the trucks. The expedition had taken a little over two hours and after a muffled conversation with Max, Böhm told the others it was midnight and they would move off at once.

They had climbed aboard the trucks and with Max and Altmann driving they had set off. In minutes they had reached La Spezia and with a minimum of noise and with side lights only showing they had gone through the small town. No one had been on the streets and very few windows had lights burning. They had cleared the town and with hardly a break in the houses they had entered Portovenere. The road was steeply inclined towards the sea and a short distance into the village both drivers had switched off engines and lights and had run the trucks silently until they had reached the end of the road that ran straight onto the sand. Böhm and Schneider had climbed down and moments later they had disappeared into the darkness as they had hurried along the beach.

To Altmann sitting nervously in the second truck it had seemed hours but it had probably only been a few minutes before he had heard the engine of the landing-craft start up and instantly Max had started his truck and had moved onto the beach. Altmann had engaged four-wheel drive, started the engine and followed. Abruptly the leading truck's lights had come on and Altmann had seen the landing-craft close into the beach with the ramp already lowered. Max had swung his truck round and driven on board without a pause. As he followed, Altmann had switched on his own lights for the few seconds it had taken to drive up the ramp. Then he had cut the engines and had jumped from the cab to help Schneider at the ramp as Böhm started to ease the craft away from the shore.

The landing-craft, with the rowing boat in tow, had travelled through the next day and it had been late afternoon before they had approached land. Altmann had kept a close eye on the position of the sun and he had been reasonably certain that the land was the north-west coast of the island of Corsica. They had anchored offshore and had slept as the craft rocked in the gentle swell of the sea.

In the morning he had seen the island clearly. Rising sheer out of the water were high red granite cliffs and nowhere could they see a place to beach the landing-craft. Starting the engine they had moved slowly south in the shadow of the cliffs until at last they had sighted a small cove well protected by rocks. Turning they had sailed into the cove for about one hundred metres before reaching the landward end where a tiny, narrow strip of beach had given them the landing place they had needed. The beach was bounded at both sides by jagged rocks and at the back by a flat-topped rock table about two metres high. Behind the table the cliffs rose vertically. Leaving Max and Schneider in the craft Altmann and Böhm had started to climb the cliff face hoping to find a way to the top. It had not been an easy task but eventually they had clawed and struggled to the top and had lain there breathless, searching the horizon for any sign of life. All had been still and quiet. Eventually they had made their way down again and the long laborious task of unloading the gold had started. The task had been slow, awkward and exhausting. The truck that had been driven on last had been the first and easiest to unload and with regular breaks to rest the bullion had been stacked on the rock table, hard against the cliff face. There it was hidden from anyone looking over the cliff or from any aircraft; however unlikely either event might be. By mid-afternoon when they had started on the second truck they had all been weary and, with the added difficulty of having to carry the ingots along the narrow space left alongside the other truck, their pace had been much slower. Böhm had called a halt long before it got too dark to continue and the four of them had slumped down on the bottom of the landing-craft. Altmann had slept fitfully through the night but in the morning, although hungry, he had felt much better. They had restarted unloading and worked steadily through the morning. By mid-day, with the sun high and hot, they had finished.

Max and Schneider had stayed on the shore as Altmann and Böhm had taken the landing-craft out of the cove and straight out to sea until they had been about four hundred metres off-shore. Cutting the engine Böhm had clambered into one of the trucks and had climbed down with an axe that had been clamped to the rear of the cab. Böhm had opened the sea-cocks of the landing-craft before the two men had slipped over the side into the rowing-boat. A few metres outside the cove Altmann had dived into the sea as Böhm used the axe to smash a hole in the bottom of the little boat. Then they had swum towards where Schneider and Max waited.

What had happened next had never been very clear in Altmann's mind however many times he had thought about it afterwards. He had reached the strip of sand first and had taken two short paces before pulling himself up onto the rock. Then Böhm had followed. As he had done so Altmann had seen that he was still holding the axe. At that moment Max had slipped. Whether it had been an accident or whether Böhm had pulled or pushed him Altmann had never known but Max had obviously thought he was under attack and lunging sideways he had swept up the Johnson machine gun he had laid on the rock. The Johnson must have been set in the closed bolt position turning it into a single shot weapon and the one bullet had caught Böhm who had been thrown backwards over the edge of the rock and into the sea.

As if in slow motion Altmann and Schneider had moved together until they had stood side by side waiting for their execution. For the first time in all the hours they had been together Max had made a mistake. He had opened fire at the two men but he still had the gun in the closed bolt position and Altmann had moved before the single shot hit Schneider. With the wet sickening noise of the bullet entering Schneider's body, Altmann had flung himself off the rock and into the water. He had known that in the clear water he would be in full view so he had swum as close as he could to the bed of the cove using the blanket of water above him as protection from Max's bullets. In minutes he had been out of the cove and keeping close to the shore he had swum south. From his own climb he had known it would take Max at least an hour to reach the top of the cliff face and once there Max would not have known whether to turn north or south. Altmann had reckoned that before he reached the cliff top Max would be thinking clearly again and would not attempt to follow. Eventually he had found a place where he could clamber on shore again. His strength had almost completely gone but spurred on by the knowledge that his life was at stake he had immediately started to climb to the top of the cliff. Luckily he had found an easier way than before and he had reached the top in less than half an hour. Once on the cliff top he had kept heading south and hardly knowing what he was doing he stumbled on until he had collapsed and lost consciousness.

Chapter Ten

After Altmann had finished speaking there was silence. His story seemed incredible but if it was true, or for that matter only partly true, it did explain the risks Potter and Delaney were prepared to take and had persuaded me to take. But there were still some things that didn't add up. I looked at Potter and for the first time since I had known him, there was a clearly defined expression on his face. Disbelief. Potter did not believe Altmann's story, or perhaps, there was a part of it that he did not believe. One thing was clear, Potter knew more than he had revealed to me. He turned his head, saw my eyes on him and in an instant the smooth imperturbable expression returned.

"Fascinating. Fascinating. Stanway old chap, don't you agree?" I nodded and turned to Altmann.

"What happened then?" I asked him.

"When I awoke I was in bed. I had been found by an old man returning to his home in Porto. He had taken me into his house. He wanted to look after me but I had had enough. That same day I gave myself up to the authorities. I told them that I had been washed overboard from a small boat taking me to France from a prisoner of war camp in North Africa. It was a small lie but it was unconfirmable and it was preferable to being involved in the gold robbery and several violent deaths that would obviously have been discovered by then. In due course I was returned to the French mainland and from there back to Germany. I did not see Max during the few days I remained on Corsica and I never went back to the island. I assumed that Max escaped with his gold." I looked at Potter.

"What now?" I asked.

"What now? Now we go to Corsica," he answered quietly, his eyes on Altmann's face.

"You don't think the gold is still there? All that happened in 1945, that's over thirty years ago."

"I'm afraid old boy that your, er, reward, depends on us finding the gold," Potter told me, a faint undertone of amusement in his voice. "As to it's present whereabouts, well now, I don't think we should jump to too many conclusions. From Mr. Altmann's description, there were thirty six bars of gold in each of the crates. We don't know the exact size and weight of each bar, but assume them to weigh between thirty and thirty five pounds each. That puts the weight of each case at about half a ton. Twenty four cases, twelve tons. Twelve tons of gold bullion. Now I know that this Max we have been told about seems to have been a very resourceful fellow, but I think even he would have been hard pressed to get twelve tons of gold off the island single handed and unobserved." Potter looked enquiringly at me.

"Yes, that's reasonable, but it doesn't alter the fact that it has been thirty years. He could have taken it away one bar at a time over the years. One bar would have been enough to start with. That would have brought him all the assistance he needed." I stopped and looked at Potter who was smiling.

"I would have thought he would have learned not to trust anyone else," he said and smiled again. The smile contained something else apart from humour.

"Suppose," Delaney spoke for the first time, "just suppose that Max didn't move the gold. Suppose he was captured before he had a chance to move it. Or maybe he moved it and then was caught. Or maybe he died. Or maybe any number of things. Whichever way we look at it there is a strong chance that the gold or at least part of it is still on the island."

"Excellent thinking Mr. Delaney," Potter said with enthusiasm. "Some nice positive thinking at last." He looked at me. "Worth a little trip?" he asked.

"Of course it is," interrupted Delaney. I was still thinking.

"How big is Corsica?" I asked Potter.

"About the size of Kent and Sussex added together," Potter answered. I looked up sharply but Potter was going on, "I know that sounds a little like the needle in the haystack but with Mr. Altmann to guide us to the starting point, we may be able to narrow the field of search to an acceptable size."

"When do we go?" asked Delaney.

"What about you Mr. Stanway?" asked Potter. "Or have you had enough?"

I looked at Potter. Slowly some of the pieces that had puzzled me were beginning to make a little sense but I still did not understand what they were trying to tell me. One thing was certain, I had no intention of missing the chance to find out.

"As Delaney said, when do we go?"

Potter's flight plan to Corsica included the necessary refuelling stop in Malta and it was dusk on the following day when we descended into the bay ot Ajaccio. The floatplane was moored close to the ferry terminal and it was not long before we were ashore and I was experiencing a few tense moments as we went through Customs with the Beretta pushed into the waistband of my trousers. The inspection, however, was only cursory and we were soon clear of that particular problem. We walked across the quayside and out onto the road where a line of taxis waited patiently in the dusk. We stowed our luggage into the boot of the first one and started to climb in.

Delaney and Potter were already in the cab when Altmann stopped short, sucking in his breath sharply. I was behind him and I tensed, fearing trouble, but Altmann was staring over the top of the taxi at a car waiting at traffic lights. The car was open and the driver was sitting unconcernedly, his fingers tapping the steering wheel in time to a tune playing on the car radio. He was thin and slightly built with silvery grey hair. He appeared to be about sixty. I looked at Altmann, the German had turned very pale and he struggled to get his breath, then realising that I was watching him he quickly recovered some of his composure and climbed into the taxi. I looked again at the car but just then the lights changed and the car moved off turning to the left and in moments it had disappeared from my sight. Slowly and thoughtfully I followed Altmann into the taxi. As the cab moved away I glanced sideways at him and again he gave me the conspiratorial look he had given me in the Cessna the previous day.

With my attention elsewhere Potter talked to the taxi-driver and his schoolboy French was sufficient to make him understand that we wanted a cheap hotel and he took us to a *pension* set high in the town well away from the centre. We booked three rooms and decided on a round the clock guard for Altmann. I drew the third shift and when my turn came to move in with him he had fully recovered from the obvious shock he had felt that afternoon. He parried all my questions and eventually rolled over and feigned sleep.

At breakfast Delaney at least was ready to tackle the apparently impossible task that lay before us.

"I take it we start where he says they brought the gold ashore?" he asked Potter.

"Seems reasonable old boy," Potter said languidly. He turned to Altmann, "Where did you say you landed old chap?"

"I do not know the name of the place but we were somewhere on the north-west coast. When I was found I was near Porto, that means we must have landed somewhere between Porto and Calvi."

"Well I think we had better have a motor car." Potter looked at Delaney who finished his coffee and left the small dining room. He was back about half an hour later with a green Simca hire car. Delaney handed a map to Potter who pushed it under the dash and directed Delaney out of the town. I was sitting next to Altmann in the back of the car and no one seemed to want to talk.

I turned my attention to the countryside we were passing through. As we drove further from the capital the view became steadily more impressive with steep densely wooded hills overshadowed by mountains pushing through the forests in the island's interior. The road we were following turned towards the sea and we were soon following some of the most spectacular coastline I had ever seen with huge red granite rocks rearing out of vivid blue water. I sat back and let the superb scenery float past. We were soon in Porto and after a few more miles Altmann stirred.

"I am not sure but I think it was somewhere near here that I came ashore for the second time. Perhaps another kilometre and we should leave the car." A few minutes later Delaney pulled off the road onto one of the few level places by the roadside. He switched off the engine and turned to Altmann.

"Where now?"

"Perhaps if we can walk along the clifftop?"

"Certainly old fellow, that's why we're here," said Potter climbing out of the car. The four of us walked towards the clifftop, Potter in the lead, then Altmann, then Delaney with me at the back. The clothes I was wearing that morning afforded no concealment for the pistol and reluctantly I had left the gun behind in my suitcase at the *pension.* I did not really expect trouble that first day but I would have felt easier with some protection. After several minutes Altmann stopped. The path we were following brought us close to the edge of the cliff and he peered over.

"There" he pointed, "there is the ledge we landed on."

"You said the ledge wasn't visible from the clifftop," said Delaney suspiciously.

"No, it is the inner edge that is hidden from here. What you see is the outer edge." Altmann was looking along the cliff and I walked a few paces back the other way.

"I think there's a way down here," I called. "Yes I'm sure there is."

Potter was looking at Altmann.

"You said you swam south, how far?"

"No more than. . . . ."

"That can wait," I interrupted. I felt excited and so obviously was Delaney. "We must check the ledge first. If Max didn't come back then the gold could still be there. A million to one chance maybe, but we must check." Potter seemed surprisingly disinterested but nodded as Delaney and I started to scramble down the cliff. It took us about twenty minutes to reach the ledge and we found nothing. I had not really expected to, but it worried me that Potter had not thought it necessary to check. Returning to the top was hard work but eventually we clambered back. Potter and Altmann had not moved.

"Well?" asked Potter.

"Nothing," answered Delaney and Potter nodded. He looked around the way we had walked. We were out of sight of the road and he turned back to Delaney.

"I have been giving the matter some thought and I am

not entirely sure that Mr. Altmann has told us the whole truth." Altmann looked alarmed. Delaney moved forward and I felt rather than saw the tensing in his body.

"Why?" he asked.

"I cannot believe that a man would never come back to look for all that gold." Potter looked at Delaney bleakly, "I think he should be encouraged to tell us the story again." Delaney nodded and without hesitation hit Altmann in the stomach. The German fell to his knees, his breath rasping in his throat. Delaney stepped forward and struck him across the bridge of the nose with the heel of his hand. Blood spurted and poured down Altmann's face as he struggled to his feet. Delaney waited until he was upright and then kicked him savagely on the knee. Altmann screamed and fell to the ground again where he rolled in agony. Potter held up a hand and Delaney stepped back. I was surprised to find that I felt no revulsion at what I had witnessed. Obviously the thought of a share in several tons of gold bullion was having a deadening effect on my sensibilities. Altmann lay motionless clasping his knees to his stomach, sobbing quietly. Potter knelt beside him.

"The true story Mr. Altmann please. Now." The German nodded slowly and tried to sit up. Potter helped him into a sitting position. He handed the injured man a handkerchief and they waited as Altmann tried to wipe some of the blood from his face. After a moment he looked at Potter and then at Delaney. He nodded again and slowly started to speak.

"What I told you before was mostly true. Up to when I was found by the old man and taken to Porto. I did not give myself up. I came back here every day for a week. I saw no sign of anyone. Finally I decided that Max must have been captured or had fallen over the cliff and I risked climbing down to the ledge. The gold was still there. All of it. I brought up four bars, one at a time, it was all I dared risk on that day. I planned to take more the next day and so on. I hid the few bars over there among those trees at the other side of the road. I could not risk taking them far. That night I returned to the old man's cottage. The police were waiting for me. Someone had reported me. They took me away and I was sent back to Germany. It was three years before I could come back, the autumn of 1948. I went first to where I had hidden the four bars I had taken. They were still there. Then I came here to the cliff and went down to the ledge. There was nothing there so I took my four bars and I left the island. I have never been back. I swear it." He stopped speaking and looked at us. I believed him. I glanced at Potter and it was obvious that he did not. He gestured to Delaney who dragged Altmann to his feet and struck him repeatedly in the face and the stomach. Sickened at last I moved forward to intervene. Potter raised a hand, Delaney stopped and looked at Potter then at me.

"I think our friend disapproves," Potter said. "Do you disapprove Mr. Stanway? Do you wish to withdraw your participation?" I shook my head.

"No, I still want to find the gold. I don't think he knows where it is that's all. Why couldn't Max have come back for it?"

"Why not indeed?" said Potter softly.

"Well, why not?" I asked angrily. "It seems logical to me. The only thing that would have stopped him would have been if he was dead."

"Ah. But suppose Max came back and found the gold gone. Gone because Altmann had taken it."

"For God's sake, look at him." I gestured at Altmann, who was sitting on the ground holding his head between his hands. "Do you think a man with millions of pounds worth of gold bullion would spend his life dealing in arms or whatever his business really is?" Potter rubbed a hand slowly across his eyes.

"Very well. Let us start from the premise that Altmann's new story is true. What could have happened to the gold?"

"Max must have taken it," Delaney answered, "there's no other explanation. Unless he knows more than he's told us." He jerked his thumb towards Altmann.

"No, for the moment let us pursue the line I suggested," Potter said thoughtfully. "Assume Altmann's story is true. Other possibilities are that Max took the gold as you have just said. What else?"

"Local people," I suggested, "local fishermen perhaps? They could have seen the gold from the sea and taken it out that way?"

"Perhaps Mr. Stanway, but I do not believe that local fishermen would have had the ability to dispose of twelve tons of gold bullion. Not without being found out that is and the resulting publicity would have been very great indeed. No try again."

"It's impossible," I said irritably. "Any number of things could have happened. Fishermen might have taken it out and they could have sunk with the extra weight. There must have been any number of rough seas in the last thiry years. I know there's no tide to speak of but with high winds the water could have washed everything away."

"I'm afraid you are thinking negatively Mr. Stanway. We are here and we have nothing else to do so let us put our minds to it."

"Very well, how's this for a positive thought. Max did take the gold. I don't know why he was missing for that first week when Altmann stole his four bars, if stealing is the right way to describe it, but Max came back sometime during the three years that Altmann was away. He came back, moved the gold and is living on it. Living comfortably. Here on this island."

"You make a good case except. . . . .", Potter broke off in mid-sentence, "why do you think he is on this island?"

"Because I've seen him." My answer brought an explosion of silence. Three pairs of eyes looked at me intently.

"Really now Mr. Stanway, what an extraordinary thing to say. What makes you think you have seen Max?" Potter said carefully.

"Yesterday, when we docked. You and Delaney were already in the taxi. Altmann saw someone in a car across the road. He stopped as if he had seen a ghost. Maybe he had. Maybe he saw Max." Altmann started to rise.

"No. . . . . No. . . . .," he said croakingly. Delaney turned, thinking that Altmann meant to attack him, then stepped forward and hit Altmann high on the head. With the preoccupation of the last few minutes none of us had realised how close to the clifftop we had remained and Altmann was nearer to the edge than any of us. The blow from Delaney thrust him backwards. One foot, trying to gain a hold, stood on air and his eyes bulged as he desperately tried to regain his balance. As if in slow motion he leaned backwards, his arms windmilling. Delaney tried to reach him but Altmann fell away. The high-pitched scream that broke from his lips ended moments later in sudden silence.

Chapter Eleven

I stood listening to the sound of the water far below gently washing around the rocks at the foot of the cliff. I made a rough count and including the MIG pilot and now Altmann, I reckoned fourteen people had died for the gold bullion. I had an uneasy feeling that the count was not yet over. I looked at Potter who hadn't moved. His eyes met mine and I knew he had already forgotten Altmann. His mind was elsewhere. I resisted the temptation to speculate just where and looked over the edge.

"He's on the rock, on the table, we can't leave him there, he might be found too quickly and he's bound to be connected to us through the hotel."

"If we go down we can tip him into the water." Delaney said. He seemed stunned. I don't think he had suddenly acquired a conscience but he thought he had seen his ticket to a fortune disappear.

"No that's no use. He'll drift around near the shore line and be found just as quickly if not quicker than if we leave him where he is."

"What then?"

"We will have to bring him up. Take him inland and bury him." I looked at Potter who was still preoccupied but part of his brain had heard and he looked at me.

"Yes I agree. How do you propose getting him up? We've no ropes, unless there is anything in the car." He looked enquiringly at Delaney. Delaney shook his head.

"No there's nothing we can use." Both men looked at me; seemingly placing the responsibility on me. I felt a small flare of anger but mentally shrugged it off. After all if Altmann was found it was my neck as well as theirs, and neck was the word. As far as I knew the French still used the guillotine.

"We'll use our shirts and all Altmann's clothes. We can make up enough to give us some kind of line." I looked at

Delaney. "Then we'll just have to pull him up." Delaney looked unimpressed so I added my own thoughts of a moment ago.

"You know they still have the guillotine in France don't you?" I asked. He turned pale, affected by fear for the first time since I had met him. Potter stripped off his sports shirt and handed it to me. I tied the sleeves round my waist and lowered myself onto the rough track I had used earlier. I scrambled down with Delaney following. Altmann was lying on his back and his eyes were open, unbelievably they flickered as I knelt over him. His mouth opened.

"Potter. . . . .he. . . . .he." His eyes widened and then closed. Whatever had kept him alive after that fall had been unable to sustain him any longer. Delaney, a few seconds behind me, arrived on the ledge. I didn't think he had heard Altmann's last words and as they hadn't seemed to mean very much I didn't repeat them. We stripped his shirt and trousers and rigged a cradle of sorts round the body. From our own shirts we formed a sling which was looped into the cradle.

"One of us will have to go first with the sling round his shoulders. The other will have to follow taking as much weight as possible from underneath." I looked at Delaney. "Which do you want, above or below?" Delaney looked at the body.

"How much do you reckon he weighs? One hundred and seventy pounds?"

"At least that," I agreed.

"I'd better go first, I'm probably the strongest." I lifted Altmann into a sitting position and turned him until the sightless eyes were staring at the cliff face. Delaney crouched with his back to the body and I slipped the sling over his shoulders. I pulled the dead man's arms round to the front and crossed them over Delaney's chest.

"Hold them," I said. I took off my belt and tied the dead man's hands together.

"Okay try to stand up." Delaney struggled to his feet. I stepped behind him and put my shoulder under the body.

"Lean forward against the cliff," I told Delaney, then I nudged and pushed at the body.

"That's the best we'll get him," Delaney said. "We'd better start before I fall down." I wasn't certain if the remark was meant as a joke but I felt anything but light hearted at the prospect of the climb. Slowly Delaney positioned himself and reached up for a handhold.

"Right. Let's go," he said indistinctly. I pushed forward taking as much weight as I could from his shoulders. We began to climb up the cliff face. The hard red rock cut into my chest and arms and even though I knew that Delaney must have been in a worse state than me, the knowledge did nothing to improve my condition. Delaney did not speak throughout the climb but his breathing, which had been hard at the foot of the cliff, was gasping and laboured long before we reached halfway. I knew that any mishap meant disaster as there would be no chance for me if Delaney slipped, equally if I fell Delaney would probably be torn off the cliff face by the sudden extra weight. I closed my mind and thought of nothing but finding and keeping the handholds and footholds that had seemed so easy when Delaney and I had climbed the face two hours before.

Suddenly the weight on my shoulders vanished and for a horror-stricken moment I thought that Delaney had fallen before I realised that the body was still there above me. Then I heard Potter's voice.

"Easy does it, I've got him. Keep coming now, slowly, slowly." We were at the top. Moments later we were lying on the ground tearing gulps of air into our lungs. In what seemed like seconds I heard Potter's voice again.

"Sorry to say it but we'd better get him into the car. We don't want to waste all that effort by just sitting here waiting to be seen do we?" I climbed wearily to my feet. I looked at Delaney who had rolled over onto his back. I nodded at Potter.

"Let's sort out these shirts first." With difficulty we untied the knots that had been pulled tight by the strain they had undergone. I put my shirt on and threw the other to Delaney. I left Altmann's pants and shirt where they were, in a cradle around the body.

"Give me a hand," I said to Potter, and between us we stood the body up. I crouched and picked the German up in a fireman's lift. Potter led the way and I heard Delaney get to his feet and follow me away from the clifftop back towards the road. We had reached the low stone wall that bordered the road when Potter stopped.

"Something is coming," he said. "Drop him behind the wall." I pitched the body forward, against the foot of the wall. Potter swung himself over the wall and waved us forward. The engine noise was louder and a moment later a blue and grey service bus turned the corner and came into sight. The driver looked impassively ahead from behind sunglasses, a cigarette dangling from his mouth. He took no notice of the three 'tourists' sitting on the wall as he passed by. A small child in the bus waved at us. Only Potter waved back. As the sound of the engine faded, Potter slipped back over the wall and removed the shirt and trousers from the body. He walked across to the car, opened the boot and spread the clothing on the floor. There was complete silence. He waited, listening, then he waved and Delaney and I swung back over the wall and with me at the feet and Delaney at the head we manoeuvered the body onto the wall. As quickly as we could we carried Altmann to the car and dropped him into the boot. Potter slammed the lid closed and turned to Delaney.

"Hope you haven't lost the key after all that." Delaney was still too tired to react. He fished the keys from his trouser pocket and handed them to Potter who locked the boot. Delaney and I climbed into the back of the car and Potter slipped in behind the wheel.

"Well now I think it might be a little dangerous trying to find a way across country. We had better go back towards Ajaccio and take the main road up into the interior. Plenty of places there where we can lose our inconvenient friend." Potter took our silence to mean agreement and he started the engine. He managed to turn with difficulty but moments later he was pushing the car along the road back to the capital at a steady speed. No one spoke during the journey even when Potter turned right instead of left onto the N.193 and headed for Ajaccio. When we reached the town he drove straight to the *pension* and parked by the steps that led to the front door. He switched off the engine and turned to Delaney and me.

"I think we should move our base from here. It may be a little difficult explaining Altmann's absence. I don't think anyone will get curious but you never know. I think we should all check out. We can go up into the mountains tonight. We'll hide the body at first light and then we can drive back and book into another hotel well away from this one." He looked directly at me. "Then we can look for the mysterious Max." I climbed out of the Simca without speaking. I started up the steps then turned and walked back to the car and put my head back in and spoke to Delaney.

"You stay in the car. We don't want someone stealing it do we?" Delaney nodded without speaking, his eyes closed. I added, "I'll pack your gear if you like." Delaney opened his eyes quickly.

"No," he said. "Get your own gear then come back and relieve me." He paused. "I want to take a shower, get some of this dirt off me." Whether his refusal was intended to keep me away from the gun I was sure he had hidden away I don't know, but I assumed the latter. I followed Potter who was already walking into the *pension.* I decided to follow Delaney's idea and take a shower. Before I did so I checked that the pistol was still in my suitcase, then as an added precaution I took the case into the bathroom with me. Once showered and changed I felt very much better and I spent some time cleaning and reloading the Beretta and arranging it as best I could in the waistband of my slacks.

I had to settle for it being concealed from casual sight rather than being easy to get at. I pulled the thickest sweater I had with me over my head and then put on my jacket. I felt uncomfortable but the purpose was served. In the mirror I looked bulky but I could see no sign of the weapon. Ready, I went downstairs and found Potter alone in the car. I threw my suitcase into the back seat and sat in front next to him. He started talking immediately.

"The man you think is Max. Can you describe him?"

"Yes, he seemed to be below medium height, but that is always difficult to assess when someone is sitting down. He had silver-grey hair. He was clean shaven and he looked about ten years older than you." Potter raised an eyebrow.

"That rather depends on how old you think I am," he said wryly.

"How old are you?"

"Fifty-eight." I looked at him and hoped that my face gave nothing away as the puzzle suddenly became clearer.

"In that case I paid you a compliment," I said, keeping my voice as light as I could. "I thought you were at least ten years younger than that. The man in the car was about sixty." Potter nodded, his mind elsewhere and obviously he had not seen my reaction. I was thankful for the silence that fell and I used it to try and marshal my racing thoughts. Delaney appeared, removing the necessity for further discussion and I was quick to notice that he was also wearing a bulky looking sweater under his jacket, probably for the same reason as me. He tossed his suitcase on top of mine and slid into the remaining empty rear seat. Potter started the engine.

"Everyone set?" I nodded and Delaney grunted. I had a sudden prosaic thought.

"Has anyone paid the bill?"

"All taken care of dear boy." Potter engaged gear and drove slowly into the traffic. He accelerated away and in a few minutes we were heading out of town towards the mountains.

Chapter Twelve

Potter drove swiftly along the road that took us away from the town. Within minutes we began to climb rapidly and were soon moving through densely wooded areas, the dark green of the trees broken occasionally by a scar of grey granite. As the road took us higher the scenery became more spectacular, the land rising steeply from the road on our off-side and falling dramatically away on our right. We drove through villages that were little more than clusters of houses nestling together in small clearings surrounded by towering chestnut trees and massive outcrops of granite. Potter drove on surely and eventually turned the Simca onto a barely visible track. The car bumped along the rough surface throwing us from side to side. Potter drove into the forest for over a mile before speaking.

"This should be far enough from the road. We can carry him well into the trees. We're not going to manage much of a grave but we should be able to find a place among the rocks where we can hide him." He stopped the car and climbed out into the silence. Delaney followed and walked round to open the boot. I opened my door and joined him behind the car. Together we lifted Altmann out and I crouched as Delaney pulled the body across my shoulders for the second time that day. Potter took the clothing from the floor of the boot, closed the lid and then led the way into the trees. Two hundred yards into the forest the land rose sharply and Potter clambered up the rise. I stayed where I was until moments later Potter scrambled back down to my side.

"Perfect," he said breathlessly. "There's a gorge ahead. It seems to be at least two hundred feet deep. We can throw the body down there. The chances are that it will never be found but if it is the police will assume an accident, that is if there is enough of it left for them to assume anything." I started the distasteful task of re-dressing the body, but I had to call for Delaney's help before many minutes. When it was done we seized hold of the outstretched arms and dragged the corpse up the slope ahead. At the top we let the arms drop and looked down into the gorge. It was narrow and as Potter had said it was several hundred feet deep.

"There are too many obstructions here," I pointed down, "and we must be sure he goes down to the bottom." I walked along the top of the gorge, Delaney stayed with the body and Potter went in the opposite direction.

"I can see clear to the bottom over there," Potter called out and I walked back to the body and together we half dragged, half carried it along the ridge to where Potter waited.

"Swing him, get him as far out from the side as we can." Delaney seized hold of the feet and I grasped the outstretched arms. We swung the body forward, then back, and finally out and down into the gorge. It was well over one hundred feet down before it struck the ground and then bounced and rolled and finally disappeared from sight into the scrub at the foot of the slope. By the time we had returned to the car it was dark and we could see our way only with difficulty.

Back in the car a hasty conference decided that we were safest staying there for the remainder of the night. Three adults trying to sleep in a small saloon car can't expect much comfort and rest. We didn't get it. For the first time there were signs of tension building. The waves came from Potter which surprised me.

Towards two o'clock I dropped into a light sleep and when I woke it was light and Potter and Delaney were out of the car talking quietly. I opened the door and at the sound they turned.

"Ah, the sleeper awakes." Potter was his normal self. If anything he seemed a little more cheerful than usual. The death of Altmann had obviously not disturbed him and I was sure that the grey-haired man in the sports car was the reason for Potter's cheerfulness and his earlier tension. I climbed painfully from the car and laboriously stretched and flexed my muscles. I was hungry. Apart from coffee and rolls the previous morning none of us had eaten since the evening of our arrival in Corsica. Potter was obviously thinking along similar lines.

"Let's make a start, we passed a bar about ten miles before we turned off onto this track. We can get something to eat and drink there." We climbed back into the Simca and with Delaney driving made our way slowly down to the main road. Turning south we picked up speed and about twenty minutes later Potter pointed to a rooftop off the road to our left.

"There it is, pull in there." The building was set low to the side of the road, it's roof barely visible. The building proved to be a small, sweet smelling shop selling most kinds of tinned and packaged groceries and a bar, with four tables, chairs and a tiny bar-counter in front of an open door that led into what appeared to be a kitchen. We stood in the empty bar and after a few moments there were shuffling noises in the back and a little old lady appeared at the kitchen door. She beamed happily and after she had determined I was the only one who understood any part of what she was saying, she launched into a detailed account of her family, friends, neighbours, the state of business and the world in general. Somehow I managed to insert enough words to order coffee and food. The coffee was typically French. Awful. The food wasn't a lot better. The Michelin guide had passed the old lady by.

When we had finished Potter leaned back in his chair and sipped his coffee.

"When we get back into Ajaccio we will book into a hotel, clean up, eat and then we can start our search for Mr. Stanway's mysterious gentleman." He looked from Delaney to me. "Any suggestions how we go about it?"

"We don't know his name so the only thing we can do is keep looking until we see him or his car," I answered.

"Ah yes the car. What was it?"

"I'm not sure," I said apologetically. "I was too busy looking at the man. It was a sports car, the hood was down when I saw it and it looked like an expensive job. The front was very low and streamlined. It could have been a Alfa."

"What colour was it?"

"Light blue and the windscreen was tinted."

"And the man? Describe him again, fully."

"Well as I said before he was sitting down and that makes

his height difficult to estimate but he was slightly built and he was low in the car although he wasn't slouching. Unless he had abnormally long legs I would put him at about five feet six or seven. No taller."

"You said grey hair. Light grey? Dark grey? Brushed forward or back, receding, balding?" Potter was leaning forward, tense again. I closed my eyes to remember the scene.

"Silvery grey, brushed straight back and it was beginning to recede. He had a pronounced widows peak." In my mind I saw the car start up and turn across my field of vision, I saw the face and head clearly. "He wore his hair long at the back. He was very tanned. He looked fit and he looked affluent, but not flashy."

"If he is Max and he has the gold he should look affluent," muttered Delaney.

"Clothes?" asked Potter, ignoring the interruption.

"Light fawn jacket, it might have been a suit – I couldn't see the trousers. Light, maybe cream, shirt. Dark tie, probably brown if it was matching the rest of the clothes."

"So we have a slightly-built man aged about sixty, grey-haired, dresses well, he drives an expensive sports car, probably an Alfa. Reasonable description to go on. We will probably have more luck looking for the car than the man. Where do we start?"

"I agree the car is the best bet and I think we should check hotel car parks. If he is staying at one we may see the car. If he's a local resident there is still a good chance he will use hotels from time to time for lunch or dinner or just for a drink." It crossed my mind that we were placing a great deal of hope on this one man but I decided that then was not the time to say so. Not until the vague thoughts and suspicions I had begun to formulate were a little clearer.

"We should check garages," Delaney broke in. "There can't be that many Alfas on the island. If it is an Alfa." He grinned, "pity we can't check the record of licences at the local nick."

"Garages will be a problem," I said thoughtfully. "You can't speak French well enough to make any sense."

"He should still try it," Potter said. "We must be as

systematic as possible on this. Delaney, you start on the garages. There won't be as many as there are hotels. You know cars. You may find someone who speaks some English."

"Right," said Delaney. "That leaves you two to cover the hotels. More important, how are we all going to get around these places? We can't manage it on foot. Do we have to hire another two cars? We're spending a lot of money you know."

"Potter can keep the car," I said. "We can hire motor-cycles or scooters; they're bound to have them for the tourists." Potter was taking an interest again.

"Yes that seems the simplest way of doing things. We will divide the hotels geographically. You take the airport side of the town and I'll take the other side. Now I think we should pay this dear lady's bill and be on our way." He rose and wandered through to the kitchen. When we were on our way again, I re-opened the discussion.

"What do we do if we find him?"

"Very important point dear boy," Potter's old enthusiasm was back. "First of all we make damned sure he doesn't know anyone is looking for him. Then try to find out if he is staying long at wherever he is. If necessary follow him, but again be careful he doesn't know he is being followed. Then get word to the others so that a plan of action can be devised."

"In that case we had better arrange to meet during the day," Delaney suggested. "Then if someone strikes lucky he isn't left alone for too long. If someone doesn't turn up the other two will know he is onto something and can go looking for him." I found that I was beginning to feel a stirring of excitement. An end, perhaps not the end I wanted, was in sight at last and I was eager to start the search.

We reached Ajaccio by mid-morning and found a small hotel in a narrow street near the harbour. By the time we were booked in and had taken time to shave and generally tidy ourselves up it was lunchtime. We all looked, and I certainly felt, much better by the time the three of us drove out in the afternoon to begin our search. Potter drove us to the garage from which Delaney had hired the car. The proprietor told us that motor scooters could be hired around the corner, and as Potter drove off, Delaney and I walked to the small garage and arranged the hire of the machines. As soon as I was on my own I headed for the main road and kept my eyes open for a newsagents shop. I spotted one and bought a street map of the town. I began a systematic search of the streets and alleyways in my half of the town. I studied every car park, and open area. I narrowly avoided being run down several times as I concentrated on passing cars to the cost of my concentration of the traffic about me. That day and the next two passed in a haze of petrol fumes and our lunchtime and evening meetings were not punctuated with very much mirth. It all seemed to be a fruitless use of a great deal of energy and I might have been bored into going home after a few more days if my motor scooter hadn't broken down.

Chapter Thirteen

Although I'm not totally non-mechanical some things are beyond me and motor-cycles are among them. As far as I could see a cog wheel on the transmission drive had fractured and I pushed the machine back to the garage. The mechanic told me the repair would take about two hours and I decided to spend the time behaving like a tourist. There was ample time before our midday rendezvous and I decided on a leisurely stroll through the narrow streets around the garage. That part of the town was in Potter's area and I had no real idea where I was. I pulled out the street-map, now creased and battered and I was studying it when from the corner of my eye I saw a reflection in a shop window. On the opposite side of the road a gate was set in a high wall surrounding a courtyard and had been opened to permit a middle-aged woman to leave apparently, from the bags she was carrying, on a shopping expedition. In the few seconds before the gate swung closed I saw two cars parked in the courtyard. One was an open, light blue Alfa Romeo but it was the other car that caused my mind to race. The second car was Potter's Simca.

I had no wish to be seen until I knew what was going on so I went back to the garage and sat on one of the work benches until the mechanic had finished the repairs. I rode off to the midday meeting feeling distinctly ill at ease. Delaney was waiting when I reached the café we used for our rendezvous and we sat drinking coffee until Potter arrived.

"No luck I take it chaps," Potter said breezily. "Never mind we're bound to catch up with the blighter before long." We ordered food and as I was eating I studied Potter. He was obviously elated although he was doing his best to conceal the fact. I had no doubt then that the Alfa did belong to the grey-haired man. I said nothing about my mishap with the scooter. Although the garage was several streets away from where Potter's car had been parked, I couldn't risk a hint that I had been in that part of town. We finished our meal and parted to begin the afternoon stint. As soon as I was out of sight of the others I stopped and waited where I was for about ten minutes. Then I slowly made my way back to the street where I had seen the two cars. The gate was closed and it was impossible to see into the courtyard so I rode past and from some distance down the street I considered the layout. The other side of the street was lined with three-storey houses and outside one was a ladder. It appeared to belong to a painter who was presumably enjoying his siesta. I wished I was. I decided to risk being seen. I propped the scooter against the kerb and hurried back to the ladder. I lifted it away from the wall and moved it back to a point opposite the gate. I climbed hastily up to about fifteen feet above road level and twisting round I looked over the wall across the road. The two cars were there. The Alfa in the same place as before but the Simca had been parked facing the other way after Potter's return from lunch. There was no sign of life. I clambered quickly down the ladder. As I reached the pavement I heard a voice a few inches from my ear.

"Enjoy the view?" It was Delaney. We stood and looked at each other. Then I gestured at the ladder and Delaney climbed up, looked over the wall and came down again in no more than thirty seconds.

"We'd better talk," he said. "Get your scooter and come back to the café."

I looked at him silently for a moment, then I turned and walked off down the street. Delaney was sitting holding a glass of brandy when I arrived at the café. He looked up as I sat down.

"Well?"

"I saw the two cars there this morning," I explained about the breakdown and my reasons for being there, then I went on. "I went back to check after Potter didn't say anything at lunchtime. I thought I might have been mistaken." Delaney didn't speak for a moment, then he nodded.

"It was obvious something was up, you were as jumpy as hell and Potter was bouncing about like a two year old."

He looked at me hard, "I thought for a minute you were in it together. I followed Potter but I was too far away to see in the yard before the gate closed so I didn't see the Alfa. I was just thinking of going up the ladder myself when you showed up." I said nothing, I was still trying to see how the discovery fitted into my theory. "For the time being," Delaney went on, "we'll have to assume that Potter is trying a double cross. He may be intending to cut us in but I doubt it. Well, any bright ideas?" I had, but Delaney was the last one to tell about my suspicions. I contented myself with a few prosaic ideas.

"We could wait and see what happens, or we can tackle him with it tonight, or we can go back to the house and break the door down." I paused, "I don't seriously think the last idea is a very good one which leaves the other two. I'm not too happy at letting things drift on. At the moment we have the initiative and I think we should keep it by tackling him tonight. He can only do one of two things, either level with us or try to get away from us and we should be able to prevent that from happening." Delaney looked at me with a trace of a smile on his face.

"Just for the record. I know that you still have the automatic. Either that or you're a peculiar shape." He finished his drink and we went back to the hotel.

I still hadn't managed to pigeon-hole Delaney as accurately as I would have liked. Not that I need to categorise people but it sometimes helps to have a man weighed up. Especially if he is likely to become an adversary, or, for that matter, an ally. At our first meeting I had assessed him as a muscle-man with not too much brain and no imagination. The few days in Iraq hadn't really changed that opinion but it had added a few things. He was harder than I had reckoned, cold-blooded and with no nerves. None that I'd seen anyway. But more important I still had to see any signs of normal human traits. No fear, no sense of humour, no interest in anything that didn't directly involve him. Only the gold seemed capable of sparking an interest in him. I had the feeling that anything or anyone that got in his way would be in danger of being trampled on, hard. I knew I would have to take care to see that I kept on his right side. At least for a time.

We both had time to kill. Delaney announced that he was going to sleep the afternoon away. I expect he did but I never could sleep easily in the day time so I passed the time by going for a walk. I wanted to think but it didn't do me a lot of good. On balance I could find only one bright spot in all that had happened since I had met Potter and Delaney at The Imperial Standard. I had started to function normally again, for one thing I appeared to have recovered my lost ability to withstand pressures and on thinking about it I reckoned the pressures that had built up over the last few days had been enough to test anyone to the limit.

I was halfway down the main street when I saw her. I recognised her easily. The hair-style was different and in white denim trousers and jacket she could have been any slim, casual, yet somehow elegant woman, in her late thirties. What identifed her at once was her walk. A lithe swinging stride that fell only fractionally short of arrogance. I quickened my step and reached out to touch her. She stopped, turned and I didn't notice any hesitation before her face broke into the wide familiar smile.

"Tom. Darling, what a small world." I wasn't in the mood for prevarication.

"Is it? We're both here for the same reason aren't we?" The smile dimmed only slightly.

"Oh dear, we are grumpy aren't we? How long has it been? Three years, and not a kind word for me?" I was about to tell her that I had seen her just a few days before, but I remembered the man she had spoken to who was still an unknown quantity, and I said nothing. I would have to wait until I knew who the hard-faced, dead-eyed man was and where he fitted into things.

"Come and have a drink," I said and, just in case the invitation didn't carry sufficient weight, I tightened my grip on her arm. The early evening bar trade was in full swing and I had to shout over the heads of three rows of homeward going Corsicans who were busily replacing the liquid they had sweated off during the day. I bought drinks and carried them over and wedged myself into a corner with Christine. Our faces were only inches away and I looked hard for any signs of change. There weren't any. She was fending off the years with all the style I would have expected of her. She looked as marvellous as ever and I knew there wasn't a man in the bar who wouldn't have traded places with me. Knowing her as well as I did I wouldn't have objected too strenuously. They could have had her. She would have destroyed any one of them.

"You know Potter." It didn't come out like a question and she didn't answer me. "He didn't find me by chance and he didn't have access to any files; I already know all that was part of the act. So someone had to have told him. Now you turn up here so that someone is you." She smiled slightly and sipped her drink.

"So?"

"So why?"

"He needed someone who knew Iraq and if possible the Baghdad military prison. When I told him my ex-husband fitted the bill on both counts he couldn't believe his luck. Then when I added the part about your slight inclination towards larceny and your probable penurious state he almost started believing in God again."

"Do you know why he wanted Altmann?" She hesitated for the merest instant before she shook her head, just enough to show she knew but didn't know that I knew. Potter obviously hadn't had time to keep her fully informed of developments. Then a thought struck me.

"Where are you staying?"

"The Campo del'Oro, near the airport."

"I'll take you back."

"No." The refusal came too quickly. "I'll see you again, another day," she paused. "It might be as well if Potter doesn't know we met here." I nodded. That would suit me. Too many people were telling me too little. It was time I started keeping a few secrets. It was also time I had a few answers to some of the questions that were beginning to burn holes in my mind. I walked with her along the road until we came to a small square overlooking the harbour. She stopped and looked at me.

"Come out to the hotel, tomorrow night."

"If I can, if not then later in the week." She nodded and

walked across to a row of taxis and climbed in the one at the head of the queue. I watched her go and counted to sixty. Then I took the next taxi in the line and followed her.

The Campo del'Oro stands halfway between Ajaccio and the airport. It isn't the kind of place you stay in if you're on a tight budget but, like every hotel in the world, it has staff who are always willing to supplement their earnings. I struck lucky with the barman. He was Algerian and although his English was probably better than my attempt at his variation of Arabic, we used his language. It was safer. After I had digested the information he sold me I thought about having another drink and decided against it. I told him not to recognise me when I came back, and left.

Delaney and Potter had finished dinner when I got back. I said I wasn't hungry which was true and when Delaney suggested a conference upstairs I appeared to be enthusiastic which wasn't true. We went to my room. I went in first, then Delaney, then Potter. As Potter stepped over the threshold Delaney spun on his heels and hit him savagely in the stomach. The older man fell and lay slumped against the door. Delaney raised his foot and I thought he was going to kick him and I moved to stop him but his foot went harmlessly over Potter's head and flicked the door closed. Potter flinched though and he had obviously got the message. I knelt by his side.

"Can you hear me?" The eyes in the lined face were filled with pain from the blow and he nodded slowly. "We know you have found the man in the Alfa and that you have been talking to him. We can only guess the rest but presumably you are making a deal and obviously we are not in it." Potter half stood and holding his arms clasped across his stomach he moved over to the bed and dropped heavily onto the edge. His face was grey and he looked a lot older than he had before. I was pleased about that. When he spoke his voice was hoarse and strained.

"I don't suppose it's any use saying I intended telling you later?" He looked at Delaney and then back at me and slowly shook his head. "No. Well I didn't really expect you would believe that. I'm afraid you are quite correct. I have found the man in the Alfa and he is Max. I saw the car outside a shop just off the main street. I parked a few yards behind it and when the driver came out of the shop he was exactly the same as your discription. I followed him as we had planned. He went to the house just off the Rue Fesch and instead of coming back for you I'm afraid to say my curiosity got the better of me. I poked around outside the house and he spotted me. Seems he had noticed me following him. He had a gun and he quick-marched me inside. I lost no time in telling him about you fellows. Didn't want him popping me off there and then. He asked me why I was after him and I thought, in for a penny in for a pound, and told him we knew he was Max and we were on to him. I tried to do a deal. He wouldn't play. Said he'd cut me in but I had to get you two off the island. Well what could I do? Didn't like leaving you in the lurch but. . . . . ." Most of Potter's colour had come back into his face and he looked both Delaney and I in the eye. Delaney was still angry but as far as I could see he believed the story he had just heard, probably because in similar circumstances he would have done just the same. For my part I raised a silent cheer to Potter's inventiveness. If I hadn't already figured enough to know that the story I had just heard was a complete fabrication I would probably have believed it myself. Delaney was the first to speak.

"Well that's over. He no longer has a choice. He shares with us and the sooner he knows it the better. Where is the gold?"

"There, I'm afraid, is the problem. He hasn't told me," said Potter gloomily, "and he isn't another Altmann. You won't be able to beat it out of him." I decided that I had better play a part in the charade so I asked a question.

"But he can't fight blackmail can he?" The others looked at me enquiringly. "We tell the police if he doesn't share. So he has either a quarter of what's left or nothing."

"Really Mr. Stanway, you are becoming quite hard." Potter said, a trace of his old mannerisms coming back. Delaney nodded agreement.

"We'll go and see him now," he said abruptly. Potter climbed slowly to his feet.

"Very well old boy," Delaney opened the door and

gestured to me to go out first, then he followed Potter and the three of us went down the stairs and out to the car.

I drove and Potter sat beside me as we drove in silence through the quiet streets to the house with the walled courtyard. I spent the time wondering how Potter would get out of this particular predicament for I was sure that, just as Potter's tale had been a lie made up on the spur of the moment, the man we were going to visit would not be prepared for us. We drew up outside the gates.

"How do we get in?" I asked Potter.

"Ring the bell there." I climbed out and rang the bell set into the wall by the left-hand gate. I got back into the car and waited and after a moment the gate was opened by the woman I had seen earlier. She recognised Potter and smiled a greeting. We drove in and I parked the car beside the Alfa. The woman who was presumably the housekeeper left the gate open and disappeared into the house. I saw a movement and the grey-haired man came out into the courtyard. Potter must have seen him fractionally sooner for he opened the door and was climbing out before Delaney or I could move.

"Max, Max, old boy. Sorry to burst in on you like this. I'm afraid my two friends know about us Max, insisted on coming along to meet you tonight." By this time he had reached the other man and was directly in my line of vision. Then he turned and pulled the grey-haired man towards the car. Delaney had started to scramble out thinking that Potter might be making a run for it. I grinned to myself, Potter had done it rather well. He was still speaking, rattling out introductions, and at the same time ushering us all into the house. The door from the courtyard opened into a high cool dark-tiled hallway with a wide curved staircase sweeping up to the first floor. An open fire burned unnecessarily in one corner and two chairs were drawn up around it. For the first time the grey-haired man spoke.

"I seem to have no alternative but to bid you welcome, gentlemen." His voice was quiet and although the accent was pronounced his English was excellent. He continued, "I suppose you require a share in exchange for your silence?"

"Right first time Max," Delaney answered. "And while

we are at it, where is the gold?"

"I've been asking him that all day," Potter interrupted hastily, "won't breathe a word. Insists on doing things his way and I can't say I blame him." I was beginning to enjoy Potter's performance. He went on, "I think he's got it hidden away up in the mountains somewhere."

"How much is left?" asked Delaney.

"Well over three quarters of it," the German answered. Delaney leaned forward.

"So if you keep a quarter of what's left you'll still have plenty." The German nodded slowly. He looked at Potter and I tried to interpret the look that passed between them. I failed, but whatever the look had indicated his next words left no doubt that a decision had been reached.

"Very well, gentlemen, I cannot be exposed to the police, neither can I fight three of you. The gold is in the mountains. It is very well hidden. It took me a long time to get it all there. When do you want to see it?"

"Tonight. Until we see it there's no deal." Delaney said harshly. The German shrugged.

"Very well." He said. "I will change."

"No. Go as you are. From now on we stay in each other's sight."

Delaney was obviously in no mood to argue and the German shrugged again and stood up to lead the way to the courtyard. Delaney stopped him and quickly ran his hands over the man's body. Satisfied that he was unarmed he nodded and we walked out into the courtyard and climbed into the Simca. I started the engine, the German sat beside me and Potter and Delaney climbed into the back. I stopped at the gates and waited. The man beside me indicated a left turn and I drove off down the dark narrow street.

Chapter Fourteen

Following the German's instructions I drove steadily out of town. I recognised the road as the one we had followed the previous evening when on our way to dispose of Altmann's body. For a moment I had the wild thought that we might have inadvertently tipped Altmann on top of the hidden bullion. A while later, however, I abandoned the thought as we passed the track leading to the burial gorge. Everyone in the car was quiet. The only words spoken were by the man beside me who from time to time directed me onto the right road at the infrequent junctions and forks in our path. From the road signs and from the rapid rate at which we climbed, I rightly deduced that we were heading into the centre of the island. The night was moonlit and from time to time I could make out mountain peaks shining white in the cold light. I almost drove off the road at one point trying to keep my eyes on a small chain of lights apparently moving along several hundred feet above us. The German, who seemed quite relaxed, told me it was a train crossing a viaduct over the valley high in the mountains on it's way to Corté; the ancient capital of the island. I took in the information with part of my brain. The other part was busy worrying over the next few hours. I had no doubt that Delaney and I, if not Potter, were heading into a trap. I wasn't sure what Delaney thought but I was certain he would be as alert as ever to danger and would not relax his guard.

I peered at the pale luminous face of my watch. We had been travelling for over an hour. The German saw my movement.

"We are almost there. Those lights ahead are Corté." A few minutes later we entered the narrow streets of the old town. Carefully following instructions I drove the Simca through the centre of the town and out again on the far side until we were almost clear of the high narrow houses.

The German spoke again.

"Turn right here, drive slowly, the road is not good." Bumping slightly the car climbed a gradual slope for about half a mile then I was told to pull over onto the right shoulder. I stopped the car and switched off the engine. For a moment no one spoke.

"Well?" It was Delaney who broke the silence. The German sighed deeply.

"From here we must walk. Please keep close behind me as it is very bad terrain. You do not, I suppose, have a torch on you?" I shook my head. Then, realising the man could not see me in the dark, I told him we did not have any means of illuminating our way. I had the feeling that this pleased him. The four of us climbed out of the car and with the German in the lead we crossed the road. The bright moonlight was now partially obscured by swiftly moving clouds. I moved into second place in the line with Potter behind me and Delaney staying well to the back. The man in front of me suddenly vanished and for a moment I thought a trap had been sprung. Then I realised the ground fell away steeply and the German had jumped down to a ledge at a lower level. I followed carefully and the others soon joined us on the ledge. For a moment the clouds cleared and I saw the reflection of water below us. Our guide followed my look.

"We are going down to the river. You must be very careful. There are many loose rocks." He turned and moved off down the steep slope. By moving only when the moonlight was shining, we managed to negotiate the slope without mishap.

"We are going upstream about two kilometres. The water is very deep in places. Please be careful." I was mildly amused at the repeated concern for our welfare. I assumed the object was to keep us concentrating on where we were walking in order that we would be less alert for trouble.

After half an hour we had become well spaced and when I turned my head I could make out only one shape behind me. I hoped it was Delaney. Ahead of me was another of the massive boulders we had been negotiating. It was the size of a double-decker bus and like its fellows it must have come down the gorge hundreds, perhaps thousands of years ago and I was pleased I had not been in the path of that one. Suddenly I realised there were three figures ahead of me, instead of the two there should have been, and, at the same instant, I stepped on a small loose rock that rolled away under my weight. I fell sideways and the fall saved my life. I heard a bullet whine overhead; the sound covered by the report of the gun. From the noise it made, a sharp crack, I assumed that it was of small calibre. Possibly a .22, that meant that the gunman would need to be close to be lethal and I decided to move back down the valley. Slowly I rose to my knees and peered forward towards where I had seen the three figures. At that moment the clouds cleared and the scene was flooded with light. Delaney was still behind me. The three ahead of me were Potter, the German and one other. They didn't see me and at that moment Delaney started shooting. The three figures ahead of me threw themselves to the ground and I hurled myself forward like a sprinter from a starting block. Behind me I heard four more shots, from the sound there were two from the .22 and two from a heavier gun, presumably Delaney's. I reached the temporary safety of another boulder and stood up slowly and leaned against the rock. Apart from the sound of water bubbling through the rocks, there was silence in the gorge. Then the moon was obscured again and I decided to move on. I stepped gingerly away from the boulder. As I did so I heard Delaney call out.

"Stanway, where are you?" From the direction of the voice I guessed he was at the other side of the river. I didn't answer. I owed him no favours and I knew that any sound would give my position away to the men behind me.

I leaned back against the rock and slowly eased the automatic from under my sweater. Holding the weapon in my left hand I crouched and felt along the ground until I found a stone about the size of a golf ball. I straightened and waited until it was dark enough to conceal my intended action. I threw the stone across the river, downstream of where Delaney's voice had come from. Several shots rang out and as they did so I drifted silently around the back of the boulder, moving upstream again. When I had cleared the rock, I waited until the clouds parted for a moment, then

I saw the German and the third man about twenty feet away from me peering downstream. I stood perfectly still. I raised the automatic then slowly lowered it again. It seemed I wasn't ready to kill anyone in cold blood. The moon was darkened and when it cleared I had lost my chance for both men had disappeared. I stayed where I was feeling reasonably certain they would be moving downstream to where they knew Delaney was and presumably believed me to be. I wasn't sure what Potter would be doing. Suddenly I heard more shots, one from a heavy gun and one from the .22 and almost simultaneously a scream, followed by a long silence. I decided to take a chance and try to move across the stream in the hope that I could make my way up to the road. I had decided that having come so far without killing anyone, I would try to get out of the whole mess with that record intact. I picked my way carefully across the stream trying to keep to the rocks. Not that I expected to keep my feet dry but I remembered the German's comments about the depth of the water in places.

I was about half way across when I found that I had under-estimated the opposition. Apparently one man had moved back upstream and I must have made a clear target for him but his shot missed me although by an uncomfortably narrow margin. I threw myself into the water. It was bitterly cold and very deep. I panicked as I went under but quickly fought down the fear of water I had always had. At that moment drowning was the least of my worries. As I floundered to the surface, the noise I was making made me an easily found target. I saw a dark shape looming over me from a vantage point on a flat topped rock. Some instinct had made me hold on to the Beretta and although my hands were still below the surface of the water I squeezed the trigger. Water erupted as the bullet smashed its way out towards the man above me. The figure disappeared, thrown backwards by the impact. I scrambled to my feet and waded out of the water and cautiously moved over to where the body lay. My one shot had broken my record. The man was dead. I felt and suddenly was, sick. I scooped a handful of water and washed it over my face. I heard a noise and turned to see Delaney coming towards me. I lifted the gun.

"Stay where you are," I told the black shape.

"I thought that didn't sound like a .22," Delaney said cautiously. He stood still for a moment and then as the moon shone out again he saw the body.

"Is he dead?" Delaney asked.

"Yes."

"What in hell's going on?" I thought for a moment and then decided I needed help, at least for the moment.

"Later, who screamed down there?"

"It was me. Diversionary tactics." I could see his teeth in the moonlight. He seemed to be enjoying it all.

"Let's get out of here," I said.

"What about Potter?"

"Forget him. If what I've figured out is right we can't trust him anymore." Even in the darkness I knew he had reacted to that. For the time being I had him on my side. Which had its advantages.

We reached the Simca and climbed in. I didn't risk manoeuvering in the narrow road and instead reversed jerkily back down the way we had come until I saw an opening. I turned into it and thankfully put the car into forward and set off towards Cortē. We were still in the town when I saw lights appear in my rear-view mirror. I pressed down on the accelerator and gained a slight advantage. Then the car behind began to catch up again. I tried going faster but the road was getting steeper as we left the old town and it wound backwards and forwards between high embankments on the left and black open spaces on the right. The driver of the other car either knew the road well or wanted us desperately. Probably both. My driving was getting more and more erratic and Delaney looked at me and then turned and peered back behind us.

"Are they after us?"

"Could be."

"Who?"

"Probably the German."

"Max?"

"Yes, maybe Potter too."

"Where would they have got the car?"

"The other man who was there, the one I killed, he must have got here somehow."

"How did he know where we were going?"

"I don't know. The woman at the house I expect. She was probably under instructions to call someone if trouble started. Presumably there was a ready made trap and we were led into it."

"And Potter?" I looked in the mirror. The lights were very close and I ignored the last question. Instead I concentrated on driving as fast as my nerves would let me on the steeply winding road. The tyres on the Simca squealed as I braked and swerved but over the noise I could hear the sound of the tyres on the car behind, as they too threatened to unstick on the sharp bends. Then the driver of the other car showed me just how important he thought it was that he should catch us. He started to overtake. As the car came alongside I flicked a sideways glance and saw Potter, his face taut and pale. Beyond him, at the wheel, was the German who was too far away for me to see his face but his silver hair gleamed distinctly in the reflected light from the headlamps.

I pushed up the speed fractionally and drew ahead again, then the other car came up and there was a harsh rending sound as the driver swung his wheel over. I looked over to my right. There was nothing to see but blackness. I suddenly realised I was mortal. I hung on grimly and forced the other car inwards. The driver eased over to his left. Then he started to come back again and I did what he must have expected me to do. I accelerated away and at the same instant he braked hard and fell behind. For a split second I thought I had cracked his nerve and then I saw what he must have known all along. The road turned abruptly to the left into the beginning of a hairpin bend. The Simca was travelling at least twenty miles an hour too fast for it. The nearside wheels hung over the edge and for a few seconds I thought I might get the car back on the road. Then it rocked sideways and I heard the stony edge of the road scrape along the bottom of the car. Then the scraping stopped and the engine noise changed as the Simca became airborne. With presence of mind that surprised me I reached forward and switched off the engine. We rolled over in the air and the crash when it came seemed far off, as if it was happening to someone else.

The Simca landed on its nearside and rolled over and then over again. Then it suddenly fell into space. Instinctively I knew that this was a long drop and I opened my door, yelled at Delaney and threw myself outwards.

Something snatched at my shoulder and I hung, swinging in space. Far below I heard the Simca smash into the rocky ground. I hoped Delaney had got out. I became aware of the silence, then from above I heard voices, faint and distant. Then they faded and moments later I heard car doors slam, an engine start up and then fade as the car drove off down the mountain.

I worked out that I was jammed into a crevice, partly supported by a tree trunk. Carefully I eased myself into a more comfortable position and gradually felt my way into a safer place.

It took me half an hour to find a route which enabled me to scramble down to the Simca and when I reached it there wasn't a lot of it left.

Chapter Fifteen

It took me another half hour to find Delaney. The car had been empty when I reached it and I worked my way round it in increasing circles until I was sure he couldn't be any further down the mountainside. Then I struggled back up the slope along the path the Simca had followed. I found him sitting half upright against a rock, he was conscious and his eyes glittered in the subdued moonlight. He didn't reply when I asked irritably why he hadn't answered my shouts. Then he pointed to his mouth. I opened it carefully, he had bitten almost through his tongue and he must have been in great pain. Apart from that he was badly bruised and he had cuts on his arms and legs and his nose had bled a little too. It took me most of the remainder of the night to find a way back to the road and when we eventually reached it we were both exhausted. I thumbed a lift for us in a truck and I avoided the driver's attempts to satisfy his curiosity. I let him drop us off near to the hospital in Ajaccio. I told the doctor who attended Delaney that we were holiday-makers and we had indulged in a little amateur mountaineering with disastrous results. Maybe he believed me or maybe he was just too busy to care. He wanted Delaney to stay but he wouldn't and three hours later we were out of the hot crowded casualty ward and riding towards the town centre in a taxi we couldn't really afford. I felt a measure of admiration for Delaney. He hadn't complained once and he sat stoically beside me. I didn't envy the man who had forced us off the road. If we caught up with him it was debatable if Delaney would give him a chance to tell us where the gold really was. I left him sitting in the sun in the main square and let the taxi take me back to the end of town we had just left. I told the driver to drop me where the airport road turned off the N193 and it took me about a quarter of an hour to reach the Campo del 'Oro and I went straight to the lift and up to the third floor. Christine's room was at the back of the hotel and it was quiet when I pressed my ear against the door. I knocked softly and after a few moments I heard her voice at the other side asking me sleepily who I was. I didn't answer but knocked again. This time she opened the door. Her expression was a mixture of anger and surprise.

"Tom. What do you want?"

"To talk."

"Now? It's the middle of the night."

"Yes now and to be precise it's eleven o'clock in the morning." She walked back into the room and I followed. She sat on the edge of the bed and looked at me wearily.

"Well?"

"Time to talk Christine. The fun and games are over and I want some answers."

"Such as?"

"Such as how come you are in a room that was booked the day after Potter, Delaney and I took off for Baghdad?" She looked genuinely puzzled which only went to show she wasn't as bright as she thought she was.

"What do you mean?"

"According to Potter he had no idea where Altmann and his friends had taken the gold yet you booked in here before we had Altmann out of the Baghdad prison." She saw the point then and I noticed she didn't blink when I mentioned gold.

"Oh I see."

"What do you see?"

"Well, Potter must have known. Known it was on Corsica."

"Yes. I don't suppose you know how?"

"No I don't. Does it matter?"

"Maybe." I thought for a moment and came to the conclusion that the chances were she didn't know very much after all. I decided to test one point. "Did Potter tell you how much gold there was?" Her eyes took on a crafty look which I recognised.

"About a million." I shook my head.

"Nearer three." The crafty look was replaced by one of real anger.

"Three. The bastard." Anger shook her voice and it was

genuine enough. Obviously Potter hadn't told her the truth and I was glad I hadn't told her how much there really was. That left one more thing to settle.

"Who's your friend?"

"My friend? What do you mean?" I nodded towards the room next door.

"The guy with the hair-cut. The one that looks like Erich von Stroheim." For the first time she looked frightened and I was childishly pleased I wasn't the only one who found the cold-eyed man unnerving. Then her eyes flickered past me and widened. I turned round and he was standing there, inside the doorway. I glanced at his hands but they were empty. I looked into his eyes and they were too.

"Mr. Stanway. A pleasure to meet you sir. I have heard a lot about you." I didn't say anything. I thought about the Beretta I carried. Then I changed my mind. I knew I wasn't going to use it on an unarmed man and, apart from that, I had the feeling I would get hurt if I tried to take it out even though he was at least twenty years older than me.

"Oh?"

"Yes, your, er, former wife has told me a lot about you."

"And?"

"And I think we should talk. Privately." He stepped back a pace and stood waiting in the corridor. I looked at Christine and she gave me a half-shrug and looked away. After a moment I went out of her room closing the door behind me. The man was already walking down the corridor and I caught up with him near the stairs. We walked down in silence and out of the main doors. He glanced at me.

"Let us walk." He went down the steps and strode off down the drive towards the road. He marched across the road without pausing and went down to the water's edge. He stood staring out over the water that reflected the bright sky.

"Let me introduce myself. I am Eugen Brosch." He said that as if it should have meant something and, after a moment, it did.

"Brosch? The. . . . . you're the one they call the Hunter?"

"Ah yes, the gentlemen of the press. They are apt to

reduce things to a readily digestible pulp."

"Then you're not German?"

"No, why. . . . . .? Oh, my appearance. Yes I grant I do look like everyone's image of a typical German officer. No, Mr. Stanway, I am not German. Indeed if there was such a thing as an opposite then that is what I would be. I am a Jew. Home, if that is the word, is Israel. And until a few years ago I spent my time hunting. With some success."

"Who are you after here?"

"Here? No, you misheard me Mr. Stanway, my hunting days are over. Now there is something more important afoot. More important than digging out the few remaining Nazis dotted about the world." He glanced at me. I met his eyes that time and there was something there other than the cold ferocity I had seen on that first occasion. After a moment he appeared to reach a decision. "The job I am here to do is of very great importance, not just to me or to Israel, it is something that goes far deeper. I think you can help me but I have to be certain. Certain of you."

"How do you propose finding that out?"

"There are ways. Tell me what happened in the mountains?" He seemed well informed.

"There was a trap. Delaney and I walked into it."

"And?"

"One of them is dead and Delaney is in a bad way." For an instant he displayed alarm.

"Which one died?"

"I don't know his name. Potter is alive and so is the man that lives in the house on the Rue Fesch." Brosch relaxed.

"Good. The other will have been a hireling, no cause for concern." Not for him maybe, I thought, but I had killed the man. I started back up the beach and I heard his footsteps as he followed me. At the road I stopped.

"What about Christine?"

"She will do as she is told. She was with Potter for money. She is with me for more money. She may try you for more still. She will not risk going back to Potter." I nodded.

"Does she know who you are?"

"Me? No. I do not think your ex-wife is the kind of person to espouse a cause however just that that cause might be. No she is in it for money alone. That makes life much simpler, don't you think?" I didn't but I didn't say so.

"I'll see you again," I told him.

"Yes, good-bye Mr. Stanway. I will contact you later. When I know." I nodded and watched him go and thought over our conversation. I came to the conclusion that between us we had managed to say very little. I wondered what it could be that Brosch thought was bigger than thirty million pounds worth of gold bullion.

I spent the remainder of that day doing some amateur detective work. I found what I was looking for easily enough. Potter and his new found friend appeared to have assumed that Delaney and I were dead. I saw them both several times and Potter's unconcealed delight seemed to me to have all the marks of a man nearing the end of a long search. He bought a few items from local shops and I spent a bundle of francs finding out from the various shop-keepers what these items had been. This and other snippets they told me, helped by a friendly gossip with a garrulous old man I saw Potter talking to at length, gave me the direction things were headed. I spent more money hiring a taxi to follow Potter and his friend back to Corté. I held my breath when they reached the point where the Simca had left the road, but they had more interesting things in mind and from what I could see they didn't so much as glance sideways. When I found out what it was Potter had arranged to hire in Corté, I added everything together and came up with what I hoped was the right answer. I didn't want to risk being seen so I told my driver to take me back to Ajaccio.

Chapter Sixteen

The following morning with Delaney feeling, if not looking, a little better, we went down to the railway station. The little red train was already at the platform and a few minutes after we were on board, with only a handful of passengers joining us, it pulled out of the station.

The line went through the town and ran along the back of the hotel where Christine and Brosch were staying. I looked up at the third floor and wondered why I still felt bitter towards her. After a few moments of inconclusive thought I decided I wasn't bitter anymore. I was indifferent and in some ways that seemed worse. The green rolling hills gradually gave way to the lower slopes of the mountains. Higher still we crossed a viaduct and far below I could see the road; a narrow, twisting ribbon of grey, hundreds of feet below. The train made several stops at tiny wayside stations where a few people climbed aboard although none got off.

It was past eleven when the little train pulled into Corté. About six other passengers left the train with us and we stayed close to them on the quarter mile walk into the town. We kept away from the main street and gradually worked our way through the town keeping to narrow, steep alleyways. I had no difficulty in finding the narrow road that led along the top of the gorge. For a moment I considered going that way but then decided that Potter, not expecting to be followed, would be using that side of the river, the side with which we were both familiar. We continued along the main road crossing the bridge over the gorge and climbed over a stone wall into the scrubby undergrowth that covered the sides of the cleft. As we followed the gorge the terrain gradually became rougher and I decided to move further away from the lip in the hope of finding an easier path.

We walked on for half an hour but, through following the easiest course I could find, we moved well away from where we wanted to be. I turned and we headed back towards the rim. As we drew nearer I told Delaney to wait where he was, then moving cautiously and for the last few yards on my knees, I reached the edge. The gorge spread below me clear in the bright sunlight, the river moving gently in the deeper sections, splashing quickly where rocks and boulders obstructed its course. At that distance the massive boulders dotting the floor of the valley looked quite normal and would have distorted the perspective had I not known their true size. Apart from the movement of the water there was stillness below. I stretched out full length on the rough ground and lay there, the spring sun warm on my back. I stayed motionless for over an hour. When I was sure that Potter was not going to be behind us I moved on, Delaney following slowly and staying further back from the rim. I worked my way down the steep side of the gorge until I was about ten yards below the rim and then began to move cautiously upstream. The going was very difficult and soon my hands were bleeding from the stony ground and from the sharp thorns of the many shrubs and small trees I had to clamber through. I stopped suddenly and listened hard. The sound was the gentle tinkling of a bell. I waited and moments later a small herd of goats appeared moving surefootedly along the slope. I waited a little longer to see if there was anyone with them, but no one was there and I moved on through the herd. I estimated that I had worked my way along the slope for a mile before I saw a slight movement at the bottom of the valley. Crouching against the slope I waited. The movement had been in the deep shadow thrown by one of the huge rocks and as I waited small figures moved slowly out of the shadow and into the bright sunlight. Two donkeys, both with large basketwork panniers hanging from either side of their backs, were roped together. Leading them was a man and, even at that distance, I had no difficulty in recognising Potter's sandy hair and thin figure. I waited for Delaney to come up to me and pointed.

When the little caravan had passed from view we began a careful descent to the bottom of the valley. Once there we were able to move swiftly but still cautiously along the edge of the river. From time to time our way was blocked by boulders and we had to scramble across water covered stones to the opposite bank. We changed sides several times and we were on the far bank when we caught up with Potter and the donkeys. I saw the donkeys first, the two animals standing patiently, still nose to tail but facing towards me. I could not see Potter and for a moment I felt a surge of fear that somehow Potter had sensed our presence and had laid a trap. Then I saw him. He was almost completely submerged in the river, splashing about at the base of the biggest boulder I had seen. It was colossal. Rearing up over twenty five feet it was more than twenty feet in breadth. From where I stood I couldn't see what he was doing but I could make out a rope which he appeared to be tying to something beneath the surface of the water. We waited, hidden among the rocks scattered along the bank, until he finished whatever he was doing and clambered slowly from the river trailing a length of heavy rope behind him. He was stripped and breathing heavily as he made his way up towards the two animals. I moved out from the protecting rocks and silently moved down to the head of the nearest donkey. I waited. Potter turned and shook the rope into a straight line from where it was tied to where he stood. Still with his back to me he threw the rope over the back of the second donkey. He turned round and saw me. We looked at each other, Potter with a flash of astonishment followed immediately by resignation. He brushed a hand over his forehead and leaned heavily against the basket on the donkey's side.

"You are a very determined man Mr. Stanway. I must admit that at our very first meeting you did not impress me. You measure up to more than your reputation. You have caused me to reassess you several times. Now I take my hat off to you." He stood up straighter and moved away from the side of the animal and lowered himself into a crouch. I didn't move from my position and watched him carefully.

"I have no gun Mr. Stanway," he waved a hand at himself, "as you can see." He pointed towards his shirt, trousers and shoes that were bundled together well clear of the river's edge. "Look there as well if you wish." I moved over to the clothing and without once taking my eyes from him I felt over the bundle. Then I moved back to the two donkeys and checked the panniers. They were all empty. I walked back to where Potter still crouched. He sighed heavily and sat back on the ground in the warmth of the sun. Without clothes his age was no longer doubtful and he looked completely harmless. I did not relax. I had been fooled too many times. Behind me I heard Delaney come up and stop a couple of yards away. Potter flicked his eyes sideways and then back. I doubted he saw anything to reassure him in Delaney's face. Potter nodded slowly as if accepting he had finally lost control of events.

"How much do you know?" he asked me.

"For certain? Not a lot. Just a handful of unanswerable questions, unanswerable that is unless I make certain guesses. Then things begin to drop into place."

"Such as?"

"Such as how you knew so much about Corsica. You knew its size. You know your way without a map. You even told Christine to book a hotel room here before we left for Baghdad. Then there was the turning where we hid Altmann's body. You found that without difficulty. And the café. You said you had seen it on the way up but it was hidden from sight, all but the roof. When we were on the cliff with Altmann you were impatient when Delaney and I went down to the ledge. I knew it was a long shot, that the gold would still be there, but it had to be checked. You were impatient because you knew we were wasting our time. Later that same morning it all began to fall into place. It was your age that was causing me the main problem. I thought you were in your late forties, forty seven, forty eight. That would have made you about eighteen when the gold was taken from the vaults but Altmann said that Max and Böhm were the same age, about ten years older than he was. Then your actions when you found the man in the Rue Fesch. That settled it. Particularly when we took you back to confront him. You worked like a team, as if you'd done it all before. You had."

"Had we?"

"Yes. Thirty years ago. You and he stole the gold and you took Altmann and the other man, Schneider, along to help." He hadn't taken his eyes from mine and I felt very tired and Eugen Brosch and his problems seemed suddenly very far away.

"Go on Mr. Stanway."

"The man in the Rue Fesch, the man who tried to kill me last night, I don't know what name he uses now but thirty years ago he was Sergeant Böhm of the German army."

"He wasn't Max?"

"No. You were Max." Potter sighed softly.

"Well done Mr. Stanway. You are really most astute."

"Some things still puzzle me."

"Such as?"

"Why didn't you find your way here before? Why go to all the trouble of getting Altmann out of prison?"

"As you have rightly deduced we were all together in 1945. I was in the R.A.F. and I was shot down about six weeks before the end of the war. They put me on a prisoner of war train going to God knows where. The guards were very poor; old men, young boys, walking wounded and that sort of thing. I escaped by just walking off the train when it stopped at a station. No one said a word and I just kept on walking. I knew I was pretty close to Switzerland and Italy but I had no idea where. Then I walked into Böhm. He was as surprised as I was, I suppose I was his prisoner but he was a very intelligent chap, he knew that the war would end any day. He was taking me back to his headquarters when we walked in on the gold robbery by chance. The guards were in the same division as Böhm, he knew them and he knew what they were guarding. He saw what the Americans were up to and he worked out a plan in ten seconds flat. I don't know why he picked me, I suppose because I was there. In the few hours we had been together we had become quite friendly and I think he trusted me. The other two, Schneider and Altmann, we took along for extra manpower. We intended them to have a share, I was to have a bigger share and Böhm was to have most of the bullion. Seemed fair. He called me 'Max'. It was the name of his dog." Potter laughed. "We decided to drive south because I knew Italy well. Used to go there with my parents before the war. In fact I knew the entire Mediterranean area. Not all at first hand, through books. I was a school teacher you see, geography was my subject. Anyway all went well until we had landed the gold.

I was helping Altmann and Böhm back ashore after they had sunk the boat. I didn't know until I met Böhm again yesterday whether what happened next was an accident or not. He said it was and I've no reason not to believe him. Not now. He said he slipped as he climbed onto the rock and grabbed at my ankle. I saw he had an axe in his hand and I panicked. I shot him and he fell back into the water. I shot Schneider and I missed Altmann by a mile, I thought they were all in it together. Them against me. Seemed logical at the time; they were German, I was English and we had just won the war. I knew I had missed Altmann and I climbed up to the cliff top. I intended following him until he came ashore again. When I got to the top of the cliff I realised I didn't know which way he had gone, north or south. So I went back down again. Schneider was dead. Böhm was gone. I knew I'd hit him and I reckoned he must have drowned. I decided to take a chance and leave everything behind, the gold, Schneider's body, the machine gun, everything. I thought that I could find a boat and come back for the lot by sea. I climbed up the cliff and went off in search of a town or a village. Instead I found some French soldiers, Foreign Legion. They have one of their main depots here you know and they were re-grouping. They were a bit suspicious of me and as I was still wearing an American officer's uniform which we had found in the cab of the lorry, presumably the gold robbers were going to use it for some of the German's involved, they assumed I was American. Anyhow, they managed to dig up an American from somewhere and of course, as soon as I opened my mouth he knew I was English. For the first time in my life I was lost for words. Couldn't think how to explain why an English R.A.F. officer, shot down over Germany and taken prisoner, was here in Corsica in an American officer's uniform. So I told them that all I could remember was escaping from the train and hitting my head. Couldn't remember anything else until I found myself on Corsica. It worked eventually. They kept me under guard for nearly two months before they had checked me out. I went back to the landing place but of course everything had gone. I assumed it was Altmann though I was never happy at not seeing Böhm's body."

Potter stretched and changed his position. "I kept coming back and looking round," he went on, "but I never saw anything, never saw Böhm." I hadn't interrupted his story but there were a few loose ends that needed answering.

"When did you stop coming back?"

"Years ago old boy, years ago."

"Why?"

"Why? Time and money chiefly. I regret to say that I have spent most of the last thirty years in prison. When I was out I would try to raise money and end up inside again. Then, during my last stretch I met Delaney." He glanced over my shoulder at his former cell-mate but from the expression on his face I assumed he had seen nothing there to suggest that the friendship was still in force. "Delaney funded this operation out of money he had hidden away from a job he did before I met him in Winson Green Prison. Anyway, I saw a photograph of Altmann in a newspaper. It was an old photograph and I recognised him right away."

"He recognised you at the end," I said. Potter looked enquiringly at me. "He started to say something just before he died," I glanced at Delaney, "he wasn't dead when I reached him, he tried to tell me something but it didn't mean anything. Then." I looked at Potter. "Go on," I said, "what happened next?"

"I always thought the gold was still here on the island and similarly I always thought it was Altmann who had taken it. That is why I had to get to Altmann before the Iraqis executed him. It wasn't until we were here and you told me about the man Altmann had seen as we landed that I knew I had been wrong all these years. That Böhm was alive and knew where the gold was. From that moment on I decided, regretfully, that I was on my own again. Now I have a question. How did you work out I would be here?" I told him about my detective work and he smiled wryly. "I must admit we took the result of the accident for granted." He coughed and smiled cautiously. "I'm sorry about that," he said. "I didn't expect Böhm to do what he did. He was very upset at the death of the man shot in the gorge. It seems he was important to Böhm. As a matter of interest which one of you killed him?" He looked enquiringly from me to Delaney and back again and it was Delaney that answered.

"It doesn't matter, he's dead, forget him." I was happy to and I was relieved that Delaney had made it possible for me to avoid telling Potter the truth, although I wasn't sure why I didn't want to accept the responsibility. It must have been conscience.

"I take it Böhm told you where the gold is hidden?"

"Not all of it. You didn't expect that did you?"

"No. I just wondered what your answer would be."

"Ah, still mistrustful Mr. Stanway." I didn't bother to answer and he nodded slowly. "With just cause I suppose. No, Böhm has the gold scattered about the island in small quantities. He told me where one cache was. That was to be my price for silence and a quick departure from the island." It seemed highly unlikely to me but I didn't say so and Potter seemed happy with the tale.

"Where is it?" I asked instead.

"Here." Potter gestured behind him. "He found this place by accident. He went swimming one day in one of the deeper pools and found a small cave under one of the boulders. He saw that it was a perfect place and he stowed a box full of bars in it. Then he realised that if someone else went swimming there he might find the cave and the gold. He found a small rock and pulled it into the opening in front of the bullion box. He had to use a donkey to drag it into position but when it was done the box and the cave were effectively concealed."

"How did he identify the boulder to you?" He moved to the side of the donkey and picked up the rope. He gestured towards the boulder with his free hand.

"He told me to go upstream about three kilometeres from the bridge and look under the biggest damned boulder I could see." He raised the hand holding the rope. "The other end of this is round the small rock. If Böhm got the rock in with one donkey I should be able to get it out with two." He looked thoughtfully at me and then at Delaney. "Equal shares chaps?" I looked at him and couldn't help laughing, all thought of Brosch gone from my mind. I glanced at Delaney and he nodded.

"Okay," I told Potter, "equal shares but don't get behind me." Potter smiled and began to lash the rope to the donkey's harness. Once secure he ran the free end over the animal's head and tied it to the harness of the lead donkey.

"That should do the trick." He moved down the rope and pulled it taut. Making sure there were no obstructions he turned and walked up the bank to the lead animal and taking its harness in his hand he pulled forward making noises with his tongue as he did so. The animal stepped forward and as the heavy rope tightened the second donkey started to move and slowly the rope rose, wet and shining, from the water. It gradually straightened and then quivered, tiny drops of moisture falling from it in a fine spray as the two donkeys strained forward. There was no sign of movement. Forgetting my words of a few moments before I moved down to the waters edge in front of Potter. I could just make out the shape of the rock.

"We had better pull as well." I turned back to Potter. We took the rope and together we heaved and pulled, our feet gripping no better than the donkey's hooves gripped on the smooth surface of the rocks. I relaxed my grip and stood for a moment.

"Wait a minute. If Böhm used a donkey to pull the rock into place then he must have pulled it in from one side not straight ahead. To do that he must have had the donkey over there on dry land. The other side is deep water, the donkey couldn't have been there."

"So if we pull in the opposite direction we should move it easily."

"Except that we can't use the donkeys," I said. "The rope isn't long enough to reach to the other bank." Potter was not to be put off.

"We can go into the river and pull from there. It's deep but we can do it even if we have to work under water." I shook my head.

"Delaney can't in his condition and I can't swim. If I overbalance in there I'll drown."

"Not with me there," Potter said reassuringly. I looked at him. He grinned. "No Mr. Stanway, the hostilities are over. I said equal shares and I meant it." I grunted and started to strip off my outer clothing. Potter untied the rope from the donkeys and slowly waded into the water leaving the rope on the ground behind him. The water was up to his chest when he stopped.

"Take hold of the end of the rope," he called. "Wrap it around your waist, then come in slowly." I did as he had instructed and slowly stepped into the water. The river was as cold as it had been before and the contrast between the warmth of the sun and the water temperature was such that the shock made the water seem even colder. As I moved deeper into the river I involuntarily gulped air into my lungs. Eventually I stood beside Potter. I couldn't speak.

"Well done old boy. Now I think it will be easier with you where you are, on the end of the rope, with me in front of you. If you slip and go under the rope will still be around you and I can fish you out." I nodded, still unable to speak. I backed away slowly and carefully. We were much closer to the rock than the donkeys had been and first we pulled in the slack rope. Potter took a grip on the rope and I did the same. Potter turned his head.

"Take a deep breath, then bend your knees until you are in a crouching position. Your head will be below the surface but we can't pull if we stand upright. As soon as you are down start heaving. Hold your breath as long as you can then come up slowly, not with a rush, otherwise you will fall over." I nodded again.

"Ready?" Another nod. Potter's head disappeared and seconds later I followed him. Beneath the surface I could see only indistinctly. Like most non-swimmers my natural inclination when under water was to close my eyes and I did so then. I pulled at the rope but the effort coupled with the awkward position, to say nothing of my acute fear of drowning, made little impression on the rock. I burst to the surface, completely forgetting Potter's warning to come up slowly. The sudden bouyancy brought me off my feet and I panicked and overbalanced in the water. I went down splashing and shouting. I felt Potter's hands grip and hoist me to the surface. He grinned at me.

"Take it more slowly this time. Instead of staying down as long as you can, wait until you are in the right position, then heave while you count to ten and then come up slowly for air." I took a deep breath. Potter did the same turning to face the rock once more. As Potter's head went under I followed. We heaved at the rope. I counted out the seconds and we broke the surface simultaneously.

"And again." We went under again. That time just before I relaxed my grip on the rope I thought I felt a movement. As I broke surface I saw Potter, water streaming down his face, turn towards me.

"It moved, that time it moved. Go steadily this time. Steady strain rather than one big jerk." We breathed in deeply and dropped below the surface again. That time the movement was distinct. We broke surface.

"This time should do it." Again we went below the surface. The rock was free and we hauled it several feet away. When we stood up again Potter was like a small boy.

"We've done it. We've done it. Don't move, I'm going under to have a look." He slipped below the surface. I stood motionless, too worried about the danger of drowning to gain any pleasure from the moment. Potter came up a few feet away.

"It's there," he shouted. "I can see it. I can see the gold." I started to move towards the shore. Potter swam up to me and helped me to the river bank. We stood on the water's edge and looked at each other, the delighted grin still spread over Potter's face. Safe on dry land, I found I could appreciate the moment. We all shook hands as if we were the best of friends.

"We had better begin at once," Potter said briskly. "I'll go under."

"No." We both turned and looked at Delaney. "I'll go."

"You're not in a fit state," I told him. He looked at me, his eyes shining brightly. For a moment I was puzzled and then I realised he had caught an old disease. Gold fever. I shrugged my shoulders. Potter hesitated for only a moment longer, then he too acknowledged Delaney's intensity with a shrug.

"Take it easily," he told him. "Only move one bar at a time. Bring them to the water's edge and we can stow them in the panniers." Delaney appeared not to have heard. He was already wading out into the river. He reached the boulder, took a deep breath and disappeared beneath the surface.

Afterwards I was never able to decide whether Böhm had laid a trap or whether fate had simply turned against Delaney. The massive, house-sized, boulder had stood in that place for hundreds, perhaps thousands, of years. Perhaps it had been unstable when Böhm first saw it and the small rock had been deliberately wedged underneath ready for the day it would be needed. Perhaps the rock really had been put into place merely to guard the entrance to the cavelike opening from casual swimmers and the millions of gallons of water that had flowed around it during thirty years had eroded the bed of the river beneath it.

I would never know. As I stood looking at the shining surface that concealed Delaney my eyes caught a movement. I looked up but I could see nothing. Suddenly I saw a faint tremble. The massive blank face of the boulder was moving, moving slowly forward. I heard myself screaming, screaming Delaney's name. Then the boulder smashed forward and down. The water surged and frothed as the crash echoed from the walls of the gorge. The water around the boulder turned pink.

I stood there for a long time looking at Delaney's impregnable tomb. It would have taken a ton of explosive to reach him. Or the gold. I dressed slowly, looking at the calm surface of the water. When I was ready I raised a hand in a meaningless gesture, then turned and walked over to where Potter and the donkeys waited. Taking the lead rein I made my way back down the gorge. After a few moments I heard Potter follow me.

Chapter Seventeen

I went back to the hotel and saw Brosch. On the way I left Potter in a bar and told him not to move until I got back. I didn't think he would. For the moment at least he had lost the enthusiasm that had carried him along for so long. I wasn't quite certain why I wanted to see Brosch. Unfinished business I suppose. That or the faint hope that somewhere along the line I would end up with something. Anything.

Brosch looked at me curiously for a moment. I hadn't credited him with sensitivity but he guessed at once what had happened.

"Who is dead?"

"Delaney."

"And Potter?"

"He's in town. I don't think he represents a threat. Certainly not to me."

"Perhaps you are right." I thought for a moment and then asked him a question.

"Did you know who he was?"

"Who he was? I do not understand." I realised it was unlikely that Brosch would know the version Altmann had told of the original theft of the gold.

"Do you know what happened in the Klausenkopf mountains?" I asked him.

"I know the gold was stolen and I know who was involved and I know that many died at the vaults. That left Schneider, Altmann, Böhm and one other unaccounted for. I have assumed all were dead except Böhm. He is the one I have been interested in. Then I found that Altmann still lived and I began to look into the affair a little more closely. I knew nothing of Corsica of course. My trail had ended in Italy thirty years ago. When I started enquiring about Altmann I soon found out that others were interested too. Potter and Delaney. And then you. So I made arrangements with your ex-wife. That kept me fairly well informed."

"You didn't wonder how Potter knew who Altmann was?"

"Yes I did wonder. I assumed at first that he was in the pay of Böhm. Then later I realised he was not. Now I am not too. . . . . .ah, wait. Do you mean to tell me he was the fourth man?" I nodded and then briefly outlined the story Potter had told me in the gorge. Brosch listened attentively.

"Very good. I do not like loose ends. And Böhm lives on?"

"Yes and now you had better tell me who Böhm is." He smiled at me but there was little humour in his face.

"I will not insult you further. Obviously I was not interested in a mere sergeant in the German Army all those years ago. No Böhm was, is more than that. Then he was a full colonel. Young for the rank of course but there were a lot of dead men's shoes to fill at the time. Not that he needed that. He was a brilliant man and he would have reached the top had Germany won the war. The very top. After all, the old guard were doomed to death or removal from office over the next twenty years whatever had happened. And among those to have replaced them would have been Böhm. That really was his name. Kurt Böhm. A very important man. And a ruthless one. He did anything he was asked to do if there appeared to be advancement in it for him. And that meant that he was personally responsible for hundreds of deaths, and by his direct orders many thousands more. Not just Jews. All races, but only the Jews seem interested in such things." He smiled humourlessly at me. "Do not fall into the same misunderstanding that others have done. We do not hunt them for vengeance. We are prepared to forgive, some of them at least. No, our thinking goes much deeper. It is our belief that so long as there are men alive who dreamed their dreams they will remain a threat to the safety and security of every man, woman and child on this planet."

"I thought the neo-Nazis had had their day in the sixties."

"You misunderstand again Mr. Stanway. The neo-Nazis, with their uniforms and their rallies were never a serious threat. Oh, they drew the attention of the press, of course, but they were never a serious threat to democracy."

"Then what is the problem?"

"The problem is that the real Nazis wanted one thing

above all else. World domination. They still want it. And to get it they will do anything, associate with anyone. Help anyone who can and does undermine the very fragile democracy the rest of us cling to. It was only recently, early in 1970, that we began to suspect there was more to the development of urban terrorism than met the eye. We began an investigation and in many instances we found links. Links between the terrorists and known sources of Nazi money. Known to us that is. The terrorists in almost every instance did not suspect the origins of the money or the motives of the men who offered it. They needed support and that was all that mattered to them."

"Why? What connection is there between the aims of terrorists and the aims of the men you want?"

"Directly there is none of course. They are merely using the available manpower. A favourite and well tried tactic. Then when the objective is realised it will be a simple job to eliminate the terrorists."

"What objective and how simple?"

"The objective is world domination of course. That hasn't changed. And you do not think that a few handfuls of terrorists dotted about the world would stand in the way of a race that tried, and very nearly succeeded in removing an entire people from the face of the earth. Think about it Mr. Stanway, would today's terrorists last long if we did not have to treat them with care and with apparent regard for their human rights? Of course they would not. They could be wiped out in weeks, days even if we had no regard for their lives and the lives of their hostages."

"And you believe they are being helped by ex-Nazis."

"We know they are, and there is no such thing as an ex-Nazi Mr. Stanway, it is like being a Jew. Whatever you do, however you change, or try to change, you never do."

"Where does Böhm fit in?"

"I have had reports on him over the years. He has been seen in England, America, Japan, several European countries and also in Africa. Always reliable reports and always the trail led back towards South America. But the trail was always obvious, so much so that we have never taken it too seriously. We felt there must be a base nearer to the heart

of things but we could never find it. We felt, hoped might be a better word, that the gold from Klausenkopf was in Europe too. Now it seems we were right. It is in Europe, right here on this island. Twelve tons of it. Less, of course, what has been spent over the years and very probably enough has been invested to replace those expenditures with interest.
We want the rest and we want Böhm and his friends. We want them soon. Before it is too late." He stopped talking and sat in silence. After a moment or two I stood up and stretched.

"Where do we start?" He smiled fleetingly and for once the smile touched his eyes.

"Böhm has disappeared from the house in the Rue Fesch. He will be waiting to see what happened to Potter. He may be having your ex-wife watched so I must remain out of sight. Needless to say Böhm will have intelligence that will identify me. Anyway I am an old man." I looked at him, he was old but I wouldn't have taken him on in a fight, fair or otherwise.

"Are you alone here?"

"No. There are others but they will stay under cover for the moment. Do not worry, for the time being you are safe. I don't think Böhm sees you as a very serious threat, indeed he may well think you could be of service to him."

"How?"

"You have eliminated one of his men and you have shown yourself to be resourceful and durable. The man killed in the gorge has been identified as a relatively unimportant man. A thug, not a political person. Böhm will need to replace him and he will not be seeking a politically committed helper. No I do not think you need fear Böhm. However at the same time you must not relax your guard." He made that last remark sound as if it didn't need making. It didn't.

We spent an hour talking details and then I went into the room next door to talk to Christine. She wasn't there and instead I walked down the stairs to the bar and consulted my informant there. For the second time he sold me information I wished I hadn't bought.

Chapter Eighteen

Potter was where I had left him but his manner had changed. From somewhere he had recovered his old enthusiasm. He chattered on about going after Böhm and trying to prise out of him the location of another cache of gold. I didn't tell him there was a very good chance there were no other hiding places, that the one in the gorge above Corté had been a permanent bait for a trap. He had brains, he could work that out for himself. I didn't tell him about Brosch or what Brosch had told me about Böhm's real persona or about the links with terrorists and neither did I tell him what the barman at the hotel had told me.

Brosch had been careful to tell me enough to keep me happy and on his side. Not that I was likely to join the other side. What worried me was that in my two conversations with Brosch there had been the seeds, tiny perhaps, of something bigger. I didn't know what it was but it was there. Whatever else Böhm and his friends might be they were not likely to be fools. Mad perhaps but not fools. They were not backing world-wide terrorism in the faint hope that one day the terrorists would gain a sufficiently large foothold to provide them with a springboard to world domination. There had to be something else. And it wasn't likely that it would be very pleasant.

I gave Potter the impression that I was in general agreement with his ideas. Apart from anything else I had to find Böhm if I was to help Brosch and if I had to give myself an outside chance of finding some reward out of the whole affair. Potter didn't seem to have any bright ideas and so I hired a car, taking care to use a different car-hire firm to the one Delaney had used for the Simca. Neither Potter nor I knew how long Delaney had hired the car for and although neither of us had been seen by the people at the car hire office, we didn't want to take a chance that they were looking for the Simca and would naturally enough be interested in any other Englishmen on the island. The car was a slightly battered small Citroën and it had a temperamental exhaust system. It kept dropping off. On the afternoon of the second day of our search it dropped off for the third time and I was on my back under the car trying to work a miracle with a piece of wire when another car drove by and stopped a little way in front of us. The car was Böhm's Alfa. I stayed where I was and hoped that Potter, sitting above me, was alert. My view was restricted and I could not identify the owner of the legs that climbed out and walked into a bar further along the road. A few minutes later the legs came out again and this time they were accompanied by a pair I did recognise. Christine was back in the picture again. When both pairs of legs had climbed into the Alfa and the car had driven off, I slid out and joined Potter who was grinning excitedly.

"You saw?"

"Yes." I switched on and we followed discreetly.

The Alfa driver was not in a hurry. If he was one of the hired hands the chances were he was taking the opportunity of chatting up Christine. He wouldn't get far. One of her pre-requisites for any liaison, however temporary, was money. Increasingly more as time had passed. That was why she had gravitated upwards in that particular set-up. I had known she had been talking to Böhm. That had been one of the two pieces of information the barman at the Camp del'Oro had sold me.

We drove steadily for more than two hours until eventually the Alfa stopped in a small village in the mountains. Called Asco, it was remote and, judging from the fact that the driver was met by another man with three donkeys, suggested that where they were headed was even less accessible. I thought quickly as we watched them mount and set off along a narrow track. If we attempted to follow on foot we might find ourselves on an impossible journey. It made sense for us to try to find some form of equine transport ourselves but that might result in losing them. I was left with a compromise. One of us would follow on foot, the other would stay behind and try to hire a couple of donkeys and then catch up with the cavalcade. The only question was who would follow and who would stay behind. I suppose there was a fifty-fifty chance I would guess wrong. I did. I followed the three on the donkeys. Potter stayed behind.

The trail was rough and steep and in half an hour I was exhausted. I was also out of visual contact with the three ahead of me but fortunately I could hear their occasional bursts of laughter and often the clatter of dislodged stones.

I had agreed a simple marking system with Potter. So long as there was no choice of route I did nothing. Where there was a choice or where the trail was indistinct I would stand three stones, one on top of the other. A secondary use for the markers would be as guides when we came back down. After a futher hour on the mountain track I was beginning to wonder if I could continue. I stopped to rest and then I heard a faint sound from down the mountain. I waited. After a few minutes I saw Potter below me riding one donkey and leading another behind him. He grinned as he came up to me and gestured lavishly with his free hand. I climbed up on the animal's back and we pushed on up the mountain.

I don't know what I expected at the end of the trail. It certainly was not what we found. I had adopted a system of stopping every few minutes to listen and ensure that the three ahead of us were still moving. At one such stop, after we had been on the trail for four hours, there was only silence. We tethered our mounts to a scrubby bush and assessed our position. We were still below the summer snowline but the others above us were very close to it. I opted to move ahead, telling Potter to follow me at least one hundred yards behind. That was close enough to be of some help if I needed it and far enough away to give him a chance to remain undetected if I ran into a trap.

I scrambled slowly upwards trying hard not to dislodge too many stones and eventually I reached the point where I had last seen Christine and her two companions. There was no sign of them or the three donkeys. It took me several minutes to find the answer to their disappearance. At first sight I thought it was a natural cave. Then I decided that a natural cave in hard grey granite eight thousand feet up a mountain was not a very probable geological occurance.

Not that I knew anything about geology and not that I cared much anyway. But it was an opening in the rock face and it was big enough for a small car to have passed through. I moved forward slowly and carefully and peered into the darkness. I saw nothing but I could hear something, footsteps and they were approaching not receding. I started back and then I heard a low voice from the cave.

"Come in Mr. Stanway." It was Böhm. I glanced over my shoulder but Potter was safely out of sight. When I turned to face the opening again I could see Böhm. He was standing just inside the entrance to the cave, partially in shadow but I could see both hands and they were empty. I watched and waited. He made no attempt to come out into the sunlight but he spoke to me again. "I suggest you come in Mr. Stanway, no harm will befall you." He sounded sincere although at first I was afraid that his quaint English might be misleading. I decided to take a chance. I reasoned that if he had wanted me dead he could have had me shot by someone deeper in the cave and out of my sight. I walked into the cave entrance and at his gesture I passed him and he turned and followed me. After the bright sunlight I had difficulty in seeing much but the fact that I could see at all told me there was artificial light present.

The passageway was narrow and inclined steeply downwards. As my eyes adjusted I could see that what light there was came from dim lamps set close to the ground. The glow was yellowish but steady and I guessed at battery-power and not a generator. I counted my paces as I walked and I reckoned I was a little over one hundred feet into the passage when I walked into a chamber about thirty feet long and twenty feet wide. The roof was a dark blur and I couldn't guess the height although the sudden echoing of my footsteps suggested it was high. At the far end of the chamber was a cluster of dim yellow lamps and three people, Christine and the two men who had accompanied her up the mountain. I wasn't all that interested in them, my attention was on the rows of shelving running down both walls of the chamber. Particularly the bottom shelf on the right hand side. Old ammunition boxes marked with the legend of the U.S.Army. I didn't know what I hoped to gain by it but for what it was worth I had finally caught up with the remains of the bullion reserves of the Third Reich.

Chapter Nineteen

Böhm was relaxed and expansive. That suited me as I had no idea what Potter was up to. He might be making a hasty retreat but as he would have guessed what I now knew, that the gold was here, it was more likely he was working out ways and means of getting into the cave without detection. Böhm seemed to have assumed I was in it simply for the money. Maybe I was but at that moment I wasn't too certain. What was certain was that Christine, having moved unerringly upwards in her personal search for the man nearest to the gold, seemed to have thrown in some words of support for me. And that worried me more than anything. It was out of character.

I looked round the cavern, somehow it seemed too regular in shape to be natural. Böhm intercepted the look and correctly read my thoughts.

"I blasted the cave myself. It was a natural fault and I knew it would be ideal as soon as I saw it. I'm something of an expert with explosives." You would be, I thought.

"How did you explain the noise?"

"I applied for a mining licence when I first came here," he smiled. "The authorities and the local people thought I was mad but it covered me then and it covers me now when I need to test weapons."

"Why stay here on Corsica?" I asked.

"Originally it was necessary but later it proved quite convenient and, more important, it was safer than moving the bullion. Most of it is still here, I find that I have to use proportionately less and less to meet the needs I have. I believe Christine has told you what my needs are." I shot a glance at her face and I hoped I read the right message.

"Supplying terrorists." I made my voice neutral.

"Correct."

"And these are some of the supplies?" I waved a hand at the shelves of wooden boxes and crates.

"Revolvers, automatic pistols, rifles, grenades, plastic explosive, napalm. . . . . ."

"Napalm?" There wasn't any neutrality in my voice then and Böhm didn't miss it.

"Yes, napalm and the flame throwers are over there with anti-tank guns and mortars."

"You seem to be ready for anything."

"Of course, there is no point in half measures Mr. Stanway."

"I suppose not." There was silence for a moment.

"Does the thought horrify you?" There wasn't any point in pretending it didn't.

"Yes." Böhm seemed pleased to have got an honest answer and he smiled easily.

"Is there a price beyond which your, shall we say, concern, will be eased?"

That seemed to need an honest answer too and I gave it with a twinge of regret.

"Of course there is."

"Good. We shall have to see if the price is attainable."

"Why?"

"I need help," he answered. "The man you killed in the gorge above Corté was important to me." I gathered from that, that the two I had followed up to the cave were not important to him and he must have read my mind. "There are any number of people I can hire to deal with routine operations and as long as I pay them well and deal, er, peremptorily with problems then they remain loyal. It is also important that they are intelligent enough to realise that what is here is too big for them to handle alone." He waved a negligent hand at the shelves. I wondered how many of his hired men had not been that intelligent and had been dealt with, as he put it, peremptorily. Böhm had stopped speaking and I thought it was time I chipped in.

"What did the other man do? The one who died in the gorge?"

"My organisation is complex. It is necessary for me to travel a great deal and during those periods I am away someone has to be here. Someone I can trust implicitly."

"And you could trust him?"

"Yes."

"And now it's time for you to go off on your travels and there is no one to leave behind?"

"Exactly."

"Well?"

"That is why you are here."

"No, I won't buy that. You're not a fool. You don't know me well enough to risk leaving me in charge."

"Of course not. No, what I have in mind is that I stay here and you do the travelling." That made a little more sense and I nodded slowly.

"What's involved?" Böhm pointed at the arms.

"I have a delivery to make. These goods are destined for an organisation in the Far East. You need not know where. The delivery point is an island in the Indian Ocean. The route there is easy and fairly direct but the return journey is much more complicated as you have to ensure you are not followed back. I will explain later what you have to do."

"What makes you think I'll do it?"

"Oh you will Mr. Stanway. You have three very desirable traits. You are poor, you are not too honest and you have an overdeveloped sense of responsibility. The first will be compensated by the payment I will give you, the second will ensure you will not be too conscience stricken."

"And the third?"

"If you do not do it and do it well then I will arrange for two, er, accidents. Your ex-wife and your partner back in England. And of course ultimately yourself as well." He looked at me carefully as if ensuring that he had measured his man well.

"Okay," I told him, "you have a deal." I was already working out how I could get Brosch and his men up there into the cave. Not that Bohm hadn't measured me well; he had, but he was slightly out of date with his information. He didn't know I had joined the other side and that I stood a very good chance of stopping his activities which would please Brosch and leave myself with uninterrupted access to a healthy share of the gold. On balance it looked as if I wouldn't have to test my conscience too much.

"Tom, you'd better tell him about Brosch." The words

crashed into my thoughts and for several seconds I tried to work out why she had spoken. Then I realised that Christine was not aware that I had changed my allegiance, or that Potter was with me, or what I was planning. For that matter I didn't know what Brosch had told her about himself. All I could remember was that Brosch had remarked that she was not the kind of person to turn away money in order to support a cause. It was possible she didn't know what Brosch really wanted.

"Brosch?" Böhm looked from her to me. He didn't seem to recognise the name and I thought for a moment that I might try inventing something to account for the spanner Christine had just thrown. At that moment I remembered the second thing the barman at Brosch's hotel had told me and I had a sudden cold feeling that events were not going the way I had expected. Böhm was beginning to look impatient and so I told him that Eugen Brosch, the Hunter, was on the island. Böhm looked incredulous and I saw the same expression on Christine's face.

"Are you serious?" Bohm demanded, "did you believe that tale?" I nodded slowly. He grinned at me and there was no humour in his expression. He turned to Christine. "What did this man tell you?"

"He said he was one of your superiors and he was checking up on you. There were problems and you were about to be replaced." Bohm shook his head and smiled again. This time there was a touch of humour there.

"Well, well, well. Describe this man." I did so and he nodded slowly. "Yes, a clear description, there is no doubt about his true identity. And he is here on the island?"

"Yes."

"But he doesn't know where you are?"

"Of course not. I didn't know I was coming here did I?"

"No. So we are safe for the moment."

"Safe?"

"Safe Mr. Stanway. The man you know as Brosch is a very dangerous man. He is my client. My only client."

"But. . . . . ."

"No, I have only one client. I supply arms to various groups but the instructions come from only one place and one man. Steiner, Richard von Steiner, former general in the German army and progenitor of the new Reich." I stared at him in silence. The trivial information the barman in the hotel had given me, that the man I believed to be a Jew took extremely non-Kosher meals in his room hadn't been too alarming at the time. A lot of otherwise orthodox Jews bend the rules on the matter of meals but I had the feeling that this time there was more to it than that.

"I don't think I understand," I said. I was playing for time until my thoughts came together.

"He was my commanding officer in the war. When it was over I met him by chance. He told me he was planning another attempt to gain world domination. I thought he was mad at first but as I listened I realised his ideas made sense. He planned a very long term build-up. Unlike Hitler he didn't believe he was immortal and he expected he might well be dead before the day came."

"What was his plan?" I asked although I was sure I knew the answer.

"Terrorism and anarchy. All over the world, every country, every state until democracy totters and then he would step in and organise the individual groups until he didn't need them any longer. Then he would eliminate the terrorists." I nodded, von Steiner had known that the best lies always have an element of truth in them. In his case he had told me almost the whole truth, only his name and purpose had been lies.

"And you're with him?" I asked.

"Of course." He made it sound completely natural and I suppose it was, for him, but there was still a loose thread.

"Then why is he looking for you? Why try to get me to help him find you?"

"Because I would never reveal to him where I had the gold. I told him what happened in Germany and how we removed the gold into Italy but after that I told him nothing."

"Why not?" For the first time he appeared hesitant.

"I wanted to retain control, to ensure that he would not move too fast." That was when it became clear.

"You mean you don't want him to move until he is too old to be a force in the new movement, so you can be the leader. The new Führer." He was watching me carefully and I realised I had let a note of derision creep into my voice. I think he must have decided then that my usefulness to his purpose was limited but, before he had time to reply, there was a sudden low insistant buzzing sound. Böhm and the two men reacted instantly. One man ran for the passage we had entered by, the second leaped for a switch mounted on the back wall and plunged the chamber into darkness. For a moment there was nothing and then a torch beam glared into my eyes.

"Were you followed?" he hissed. I couldn't see any point in playing games and anyway I didn't want to be the cause of Potter being killed.

"Yes," I told him. "It's Potter, he was with me. What caused the buzzer to sound, a trip wire?"

"Not exactly, just a pressure pad. You're sure it's only Potter?"

"Who else could there be?" As I said it I knew there was an answer to that and so did he. As if to confirm the thought the buzzer sounded again.

He snapped off the torch.

"That's a second man," he said softly, "or Potter going out again."

Then the buzzer sounded again and that settled matters. In the darkness I eased the Beretta from my waistband, I wasn't sure which way things would go but I had already picked sides. I was on my own again.

I backed away, moving softly until I felt one of the shelves behind me. My fingers followed the outlines of a box and I explored the inside in case there was anything that might help. There was. The box contained grenades. I took two. I could hear breathing in the darkness in front of me and I reversed the Beretta. I was ready to use it as a club when I caught a faint smell that spelled woman and I reached out and touched Christine. I felt the answering pressure of her fingers and then she brought her lips close to my ear.

"The donkeys," she breathed. I don't know what made her decide to throw in with me, probably she had calculated that the way things were going lives were going to be lost and that amongst those present I was the least dangerous to her. In any event I didn't worry about it then, I was too busy thinking about what she had said. I had forgotten about the donkeys I had followed up to the cave. They hadn't been left outside and they weren't in the cave. That meant there was another cave and there might be another way out. Obviously Bohm and the others knew if there was but I couldn't very well ask them.

"Where did they go?" I whispered into Christine's ear.

"Just by the tunnel we came through, on that back wall, there's another chamber."

"Is there a way out from there?"

"I don't know." I moved slowly towards the outer end of the chamber with Christine holding on to my shirt. Ahead of us there was a sudden explosion of gunfire. Echoes round the confined space made an accurate count impossible but I reckoned at least six shots and from a mixture of calibres, certainly two, possibly three. Then there was silence again and as my ears recovered from the blast of noise I heard breathing from close ahead. I still held the Beretta by the barrel and I decided to keep it that way, not that I still harboured any thoughts about not killing, it just seemed less likely to draw shots in my direction.

I waited, tense and then I swung the weapon in the direction of the noise. From the soft thud as the blow landed I guessed I had struck a shoulder and the grunt of pain told me the target was hurt. I reached out my free hand and found a man's face. It was Potter, the moustache left no doubt.

"Potter, it's me," I hissed.

"Stanway old chap," the familiar voice whispered, "whose side are you on?"

"Mine."

"Mind if I join you?" I didn't think I had a lot to lose.

"Okay. There's another chamber somewhere, maybe another way out. How many are with you?"

"Four, including Brosch. Afraid I brought him here, seems to have been an error." I didn't answer that, it seemed the safest course. I guided Potter's hand to Christine's so we all knew where we were. I led the way again until I reached the wall of the chamber.

There was another burst of gunfire and this time I was able to locate it as I could see flashes from the tunnel we had entered by. I felt along the wall and in moments I found an opening. Inside I could hear muffled noises and from the smell I reckoned we were in the donkey's stable. I pulled Potter and Christine in behind me.

"Have you any matches?" I asked.

"I've got my lighter," Christine answered and after a moment she pressed it into my hand. I lit it and snapped the flame off almost at once. No one fired at us so I tried again, this time for a little longer. The three donkeys were there and that was all. I tried a light again for longer still and the flame wavered slightly. There was a movement of air in the chamber and it was towards the way we had entered. That seemed to mean there was an air passage but whether it would be big enough for us was another matter. Potter fumbled with the ropes tethering the animals.

"What are you doing?"

"If there's a way out they'll find it just as well as us, probably faster, more important the noise they make will cover us."

"Okay." I heard the sound of Potter's hand slapping the side of the three donkeys and they clattered past me and I followed them. Behind me I could hear the others and behind them more shots were fired. I said a silent prayer that we wouldn't have to go back that way. It didn't sound very healthy.

Chapter Twenty

It wasn't all that healthy outside either. The secondary opening reached the surface slightly more than ninety degrees round the mountain from the main entrance. Measured in fact it was less than one hundred feet but it might have been a million miles away. We had approached the main entrance across a small clear level area at the end of the track up the mountainside. The opening we left by was bounded on both sides and below by loose scree covered by a light sprinkling of snow. An experienced mountaineer would have thought twice about tackling it. Thought twice and decided not to in all probability. There was a small space, directly in front of the aperture we had emerged from, that was distinctly overcrowded with three humans and three donkeys. Potter's idea to send the animals ahead of us had backfired and my attempts to persuade them back inside failed. They proved to be as stubborn as their reputation held them to be although, in the circumstances, I can't say I blamed them. I asked Potter what had happened.

"I'm almost ashamed to admit it old boy but I tried a little double-dealing." It seemed he was remaining true to form to the bitter end. "Brosch contacted me, told me he wanted my help and I agreed. He offered me a fair price. When you left me behind in Asco I telephoned him. Then when you went into the cave I went back to the village and waited for him. I thought something might be amiss when he showed up, in a helicopter, with some very unappetising looking fellows. They were German and that made me wonder about him." I interrupted and told him who Brosch really was and also something of what was going on. He nodded. "That explains a lot. When we reached the cave they made me go in first, in case there was a trap. Very unsporting."

"What happened?"

"I was going down the passage when I heard a noise, I

guessed I'd activated a warning. I felt around me and there was a ledge about shoulder height, I pulled myself up on that and waited. Someone came up out of the cave, passed me and I climbed down and carried on. You heard the shots. Obviously your friends met mine."

From behind us in the cave I could hear muffled reports and there were others obviously from around the mountain.

"Brosch, Steiner to give him his real name, must have Böhm pinned down inside."

"Why doesn't Böhm come out this way?" Christine asked.

"Because he knows there's no way down from here. He's safer where he is and he has all the fire power."

"Fire power?" Potter asked. I told him about the arsenal Böhm had in the chamber in the mountain. At the same time I remembered the grenades but for the moment I couldn't think of a way to use them. Abruptly one of the donkeys decided it had had enough for one day and it stepped into the scree. The loose surface slid away and the animal sat down on its rear end and, like a cartoon character, it slid down the slope in a flurry of noise and stones. Sixty feet below it reached solid ground and stood up, twitched its ears and trotted off in the direction of home. I looked at its companions, they were moving uneasily and it was obvious they were on the verge of following.

"Quickly, grab hold," I pushed Christine and Potter. "Hand on to the tail, the bridle." They had both seen the possibility of a way out and Christine didn't hesitate. Surprisingly Potter did.

"What about you old boy?"

"Don't worry about me, I'll make it." I grinned at him, I didn't feel particularly confident but I wasn't ready to relinquish my toehold on a fortune. It had also occurred to me that Brosch and, for that matter, Böhm might have reinforcements in the offing. If I went down and tried to pick off the winner of the battle at the cave at my leisure I might very well find myself in trouble. If I had reasoned it out then reinforcements would have caused me trouble whatever I did but my reasoning wasn't at it's best. Gold, in large quantities, has that effect on people. Potter reached out and shook my hand which ought to have seemed ridiculous in the circumstances but oddly enough it didn't.

With some encouragement from me first one and then the other of the two donkeys slid noisily down the scree with their awkward and unwelcome riders. They made it and Potter waved briefly. Suddenly more shots were fired and I saw Potter dive for cover pulling Christine with him. They had been heard by Steiner's men and lower down they were in view and someone had thrown off a couple of snap shots. I waited tense, then I heard a shout and there were no more shots fired in that direction. Steiner must have recognised them and realised they were not important to him anymore. It also meant he now knew there was another way out and he would be sending someone to try and cover that exit. The logical place to do that from was the bottom of the scree where Potter was but Steiner wouldn't know how difficult the terrain was higher up. He would probably first send someone to try and get round to where I was. I doubted he would make it but he might get far enough to have me in range. I looked down and decided that on my own I didn't fancy my chances. I had already discounted a sideways move. That left upwards.

As far as I could see the face of the mountain was smoother above the opening and although still covered with snow, there was not much loose stone. The worst thing about it was that it was steeper than below. Unfortunately I didn't seem to have a lot of choice, as I had already decided I certainly wasn't going back inside. I was still holding the Beretta and I pushed it back into the waistband of my trousers and began to scramble slowly and painfully up towards the peak. The grenades in my jacket pockets clumped alarmingly against the rock and I kept repeating to myself that they were harmless. For the first time since I had reached the snowline, although the sun still shone, I began to feel cold. I realised that the wind was blowing more strongly than it had before and snow, disturbed by my hands, was whipped up, the particles biting sharply into my face.

I had no clearly formed plan in mind. Primarily I wanted to be out of that particular spot, but as I struggled upwards I realised that if I could work my way over to the right I might be able to cover both entrances to the cave. It took me almost half an hour to reach a point where I could see both entrances and be in no immediate danger of falling. Below me I could see the clearing in front of the main entrance and from the occasional shots I knew there were at least two gunmen among the rocks opposite the opening. Further down I could see another man in the position I had thought of earlier. He was covering both entrances from below. It was about then that I realised I wasn't in a very good position after all. I could see them and if they chose to look up, as they would if I opened fire, they would see me. There were three of them with, presumably, three guns. I had the Beretta, not fully loaded, and two grenades. Inside the cave Böhm had enough weaponry to start a small war. On balance I was not likely to come out of things very well.

That was when Böhm counter-attacked and unwittingly redressed the balance in my favour. I had wondered why he hadn't used the facilities he had at his disposal, but then it was always possible that the weaponry was disassembled. In any event when he did attack he made up for the delay. He used the most searching, the most obscene weapon he had. A flame-thrower. The hissing roaring jet of flames shot out of the main exit and billowed in a vivid yellow and orange cloud into and around the rocks where I had seen movements before. The result was appalling. Two figures came out from the rocks, flames enveloping them as they tried to run away. But they couldn't because they were the flames. What made it all seem worse was the fact that, unbelievably, there was no sound, no screams of pain, just a silent desperate, unavailing bid to escape. And then there was a sound, the hissing roar of the jet of napalm came again and the two men ceased to be men and became charred, flame-licked monsters, still, somehow erect. Then they fell, slowly, like trees being felled and they rolled downwards burning until they were brought to a standstill by the scrubby trees they now so closely resembled.

That was when I decided what to do. Carefully because I could not afford to make a mistake I took out one of the grenades and removed the safety pin. I tried to remember all I had known about them, I released the grip and counted slowly and then I tossed the grenade out and downwards. It landed squarely in the opening and rolled back, inwards. The explosion was violent although muffled and the mountainside trembled, then it was still. I began to make my way to the secondary opening. Below I could see the remaining man, the one who had gone down to cover that exit. He waved to me. It was von Steiner although I still thought of him as Brosch. He must have thought I was still on his side. It took me longer to get back, the snow seemed harder and more slippery, probably as the temperature had fallen in the wind. I stayed above the hole, I wasn't risking being in the firing line of Böhm's flame-thrower, if anyone inside was still alive. I shouted his name. Faintly I heard his voice.

"Stanway, is that you?"

"Yes. Come out Böhm. All of you."

"There is only me, the others are dead, one shot, one by the explosion. The grenade, was that you?"

"Yes."

"Have you another?" I hesitated.

"No." There was silence and I knew he hadn't missed my hesitation. Then I heard him moving. Hearing my voice from inside the cave he couldn't have known I was above him and he moved into my sight. He relied on the angle of the rock face for protection, but instead it gave me a clear view of him, and what he carried. He had the flame-thrower in his hands, the napalm containers strapped to his back, and from his movements there was little doubt he meant to use it again. And the target was to be me.

I took the remaining grenade from my pocket and then put it back again. There would be a time lag between the grenade striking the ground and the explosion. Böhm could use that gap to do one of two things, he could jump to safety, either into the cave or take a chance down the scree, or he could use the time to fire off a jet of burning napalm at me. I wasn't prepared to take the chance that he would use that time for self-preservation. I eased the Beretta out and released the safety catch. Then Brosch-Steiner took a hand.

He opened fire on Böhm, using, as far as I could judge, a high-powered automatic rifle. It seemed he wasn't a very good shot as the bullet struck the snow covered rocks below and to the left of where Böhm stood. Böhm disappeared back out of sight and I tried to decide what to do next.

Once again the decision was taken for me. Böhm must have been very busy in the cavern after we had got out. In addition to setting up the flame-thrower he had prepared one of the heaviest weapons he had. I wasn't sure whether it was a mortar or an anti-tank gun or something else entirely. Whatever it was something whistled from the opening with more velocity than was needed and the projectile crashed into the trees well below the snow-line with a shattering explosion. I saw movement in the scrubby trees that concealed Potter and Christine and Brosch-Steiner. It didn't take much intelligence to deduce that Böhm would rapidly adjust his aim. I had to do something about it and it seemed that the remaining grenade was the only answer. I slipped it from my pocket and released the pin and dropped it in another hopeful looping lob. I was as lucky with the second throw as I had been with the first. If what happened next could be described as lucky.

The grenade bounced and rolled inwards exactly as before and the roar as it exploded was followed by a rumbling crash and then unexpectedly a second explosion. I don't know what happened but a reasonable guess was that the grenade had started a rock fall and that, at the same time, Böhm had fired his weapon again, his shell striking and exploding against the fall. Then the mountain trembled and instantly I knew that somehow the whole arsenal had exploded. When the sound of the explosion reached my ears I was already being thrown outwards from my perch. I hit the rock face again, below the place where the opening had been, and I was aware that I was surrounded by flying stones, some small, some large and it was one of the large stones that hit me in the face. I saw it coming and there was nothing I could do about it. As I blacked out I was, absurdly, dividing the value of the bullion by the survivors; me, Potter, Christine and Brosch-Steiner.

Chapter Twenty One

When I swam up out of unconsciousness I was lying on my back on soft ground. I tried to get up and I couldn't. My legs were tied together and I struggled up to my elbows and looked around. I was alone. I looked down at my legs and I could see they were bound together with strips of cloth and along my left leg was a short length of timber broken from a tree branch. I realised I had a broken leg moments before I began to feel the waves of pain.

"Hello old chap, woken up at last have you?" It was Potter, he was coming out of the trees over to my left.

"If it doesn't sound ridiculous, what happened?"

"What do you remember?"

"The explosion and my flying through the air. Then something hit me."

"Miracle you survived at all, old boy. You came off that mountain like one of those Mexican divers. Then the rocks caught up with you and I thought you'd had it. When the rocks stopped falling I came over and found you. You took one in the face and your leg was broken. Apart from that you seem alright."

"Where's Christine?"

"Further down the mountain. It's safer down there."

"And Brosch?"

"A rock the size of a refrigerator hit him in the chest. He's over there, I don't think he'll last long. Internal bleeding and I can't risk moving him." I didn't ask why he hadn't gone for help. I wasn't sure I wanted to hear the reply, he was probably calculating the division of the gold if Brosch died.

"Help me up," I said instead. He pulled me up and I leaned on him as he took me to see the wounded German. He was lying half-propped against a tree, his face pale and drawn. His eyes were open and they watched us approach. They were no longer cold and hard, they were filled with pain and something more. He was dying and he knew it.

"Mr. Stanway, I congratulate you, you have a quality I admire. You are a survivor. You too Mr. Potter, your search has been as long as mine, longer even. And now it is yours, all yours. If you can reach it." I looked at him without understanding and then his eyes moved upwards and I followed his look. The top of the mountain had changed it's shape. I looked at Potter and he nodded slowly.

"Yes, I'm afraid so. The explosion has pulled down all the face above the cavern. The bullion is buried, inaccessible. Gone forever."

"Unfortunate, gentlemen, unfortunate." The German coughed and blood trickled onto his chin. He started to speak again but the coughing didn't stop and neither did the blood. And then the coughing did stop and after a moment the blood stopped too. He was dead.

It took us a long time to reach the village and it was well past mid-night before we were back at the car. Potter had found one of the donkeys and he had helped me to drape myself face down over its back. He walked and part way down the trail we found Christine sitting waiting. Waiting to see who had survived. She didn't seem to like the choice fate had made.

We didn't see anyone in the village. Someone must have heard the explosion but they probably thought the mad miner was at it again, or they may have thought the Foreign Legion were exercising in the area. Whatever the reason no one came out to stare at us.

I had passed out twice on the donkey and I blacked out again in the car on the way back to Ajaccio. Potter took me to the hospital and I saw the same doctor who had treated Delaney. I couldn't have been in better hands; as with Delaney he was not interested in me as an individual but as a subject for his skill.

Two days later Potter came to see me.

"How are you old boy?"

"Well enough."

"When are they letting you out?"

"Today. In a couple of hours in fact."

"What are you planning to do?"

"I'm going back to England on the first aircraft I can get

on."

"Ah, yes, had enough eh?" I looked at him curiously.

"Haven't you?" He grinned slightly and shook his head.

"Afraid not old chap. I'm planning to have a go at digging my way into the chambers." I couldn't think of anything to say that would suit the occasion so instead I said nothing. After a few minutes he went and I levered myself out of bed and hobbled over to the window awkwardly on my plaster encased leg.

Below me on the road outside the hospital I saw Potter walk across to a Landrover. In the back were tools, pickaxes, shovels and piles of boxes and cartons. I shook my head, half in admiration, half in regret. The Landrover started up and turned to head out of town and I could see Potter had a companion. Christine. I wondered how long she would stay with him in his hopeless self-appointed task. Not long if past performance was anything to go by.

I was fastening my seat belt as the Air-France jet began its approach to Heathrow Airport and looking forward to a drink and the long explanation to Tony Miller, when it crossed my mind that Potter's task might not be entirely hopeless. Then I shook my head; that kind of thinking had brought me enough trouble already. Still it was something to think about in the long winter evenings and it wouldn't do me any harm to have a holiday the following summer. A holiday on a golden island in the Mediterranean.